Edward Kennard

A Crack County

A novel

Edward Kennard

A Crack County
A novel

ISBN/EAN: 9783337052300

Printed in Europe, USA, Canada, Australia, Japan

Cover: Foto ©Andreas Hilbeck / pixelio.de

More available books at **www.hansebooks.com**

A Novel.

BY

MRS. EDWARD KENNARD,

Author of

"KILLED IN THE OPEN," "THE GIRL IN THE BROWN HABIT,"
"A REAL GOOD THING," ETC., ETC.

IN THREE VOLUMES.

VOL. I.

LONDON:

F. V. WHITE & CO.,

31, SOUTHAMPTON STREET, STRAND, W.C.

1888.

CONTENTS.

—·—

A CRACK COUNTY.

CHAPTER I.

A VERY SELECT HUNT.

THE real name of the Hunt was the Morbey Anstead.

But in sporting circles it was always called " The Mutual Adoration." In fact, so generally was this latter appellation employed that most people were apt to forget it possessed any other.

As the " Mutual Adoration " they were known far and wide, but although there was not a finer country in Great Britain than that which they had the good fortune to hunt, the pack was not popular with strangers. Year after year the same faces might be seen at covert side; very few new ones ever appeared amongst them.

Rich young men with large studs, plenty of money and a desire to get rid of it, such as are invariably welcome in most country places; officers spending their long leave; fathers of families, hampered by the care of so many young ones, but as keen about hunting as ever, did not choose Morbey Anstead as their head-quarters.

This was the more remarkable, because the town itself offered many advantages. It was clean, healthy, well situated on the top of a breezy hill, and moreover abundantly stocked with good inns and excellent stabling. But alas! both inns and stables stood empty.

And yet people who had been to Morbey Anstead once, never complained of it as a bad place from which to enjoy the chase. On the contrary, they praised it highly; but what they *did* complain of very loudly and very bitterly, were the manners of the "Mutual Adoration" Hunt. As strangers they went amongst that fastidious crew and as strangers they came away, feeling that if they hunted from Morbey Anstead all their days, such they would remain. For after riding behind these exclusives the whole season, you were but too apt to find your existence overlooked just as much at the end of it as at the beginning.

Now there is no denying the fact that folks don't like this sort of thing; and various were the remarks made ; often not altogether of a laudatory description. It may be vanity, but it is also human nature to desire some recognition from your fellow-creatures.

"Upon my soul, we might just as well be so much dirt," quoth one incensed sportsman.

"Dirt ! say pitch," answered his companion. "For they *do* condescend to make the acquaintance of Mother Earth now and again."

" Ha, ha! very good, very good," said a third. " The worst of it is, though, after a bit a fellow begins to wonder what the deuce is the matter with him, when he goes out hunting and not a soul will say a word, or recognize his presence. He fancies that the fault must lie with himself, and that ain't by any means a pleasant feeling."

" True," put in a fourth. " But when you have seen a little more of the M. A.'s, then you turn round and enquire what the devil is the matter with *them?* "

" They are so confounded exclusive! " sighed the son of a grocer, who had taken to hunting, thinking he would get elevated into County society.

" My dear fellow," said the first speaker, contemptuously, " the whole thing lies in a nut-shell, and I for one say that the Mutual

Adorationites are more to be pitied than blamed. They have only one idea in their heads, and that's hunting. They can think of nothing else, talk of nothing else. Their brains get brutalized, and their manners suffer in consequence. My own belief is that this rudeness and reticence proceeds from a very simple cause. They are not wise enough to know any better;" and so on, and on *ad infinitum*, for the malcontents were very numerous.

This remark happened to get round to the ears of those for whom it was not intended. Such remarks always do. They travel with marvellous rapidity, and generally land in the precise quarter where they are calculated to do the largest amount of mischief.

The indignation of the Mutual Adorationites was quite comical.

Not know any better indeed! They flattered themselves they knew a very *great deal* better than to take up with every Tom, Dick and Harry who put on a red coat and chose to appear outside a horse.

They liked to know who people were, where they came from, how far their ancestors could be traced, and in what sort of society they moved, before jumping down their throats, and even then there was no hurry. It was always better to take plenty of time to consider about these things, for fear of making a mistake. It would never answer for them—the Mutual Adorationites—to incorporate a person into their select body, and then find that that person would not do ! There had been such a case on record, and every M. A. to a man was agreed it must never happen again. And to do them justice, this was their first and last error of familiarity. Under the circumstances, it will not perhaps be difficult to understand how it came about that the Hunt was a small one. It was still further reduced by being divided and split up into sections.

First came the "riff-raff"—the kind of folks whom the M. A.'s saw year after year, and ignored entirely. They might be very good fellows in their way, but, to use their own expressive language, "they did not tumble to them."

Fortunately for these gentlemen—who constituted the larger portion of the field—they were able to form a society of their own, which enabled them to survive the frigidity of their fellow Nimrods.

Then came the "Half-and-halfers"—people whom the Mutual Adorationites, for various reasons, did not wholly condemn, even while they they could not altogether accept.

These were tolerated, passively and in a luke-warm fashion, which proved more galling to some than direct avoidance.

On the recurrence of each hunting

season, and after an absence probably of several months, they would find themselves greeted by a careless nod and a muttered "How do." Or if the M. A. happened to be in an unusually amiable and loquacious mood, he might even go the length of saying, "Fine day. Looks like a scenting morning."

But this was quite an oratorical effort, and generally meant, "There! I've done the civil to you, because you are a covert owner, but for goodness sake don't expect me to go talking to you any more to-day."

As a matter of fact, no real M. A. would ever unbend so far as to be seen carrying on a conversation with a "Half-and-halfer." They kept their conversations and their ideas for themselves. They were too precious, or perhaps too scarce to be showered upon the world of "outsiders." Anyhow, they were not scattered like pearls before swine.

The *bonâ-fide* Mutual Adorationites did not number more than a dozen.

When they went a-hunting they formed a coterie apart.

They rode together, talked or rather kept silence together, and jogged home together.

All the rest of the field were made to feel themselves without the pale.

But the M. A.'s, for all their exclusiveness, were not jovial. There was none of that friendly, harmless, good-natured chatter going on amongst them which is one of the characteristic features of most covert sides, and often is carried to too great an excess.

Occasionally one of their number would jerk out an observation, and his companion would grunt out a reply. But there was no mirth, or jollity ; no fun and geniality.

They were stately, and solemn, and dull to a degree. As for a joke—but there !

they never condescended to anything half so vulgar or so abominably plebeian. A joke would have been considered bad form.

The mere fact of riding about in each other's company seemed to afford a kind of sedate pleasure. Any interchange of thought was quite superfluous.

Unfortunately, their very exclusiveness rendered them few in numbers.

Death and absence had thinned their ranks to such an extent that at the period when our story commences, there were not more than a dozen legitimate Mutual Adorationites left. Still, they sufficed to maintain the character of the Hunt, and effectually drove away any rash stranger, who, tempted by the beauty of the country, and the convenience of Morbey Anstead as a sporting centre, took it into his head to come out with the hounds.

First and foremost ranked the master, Lord Littelbrane.

He was a small, fair, colourless, insignificant-looking man, about forty-five years of age, with a drab complexion, and hair to match. He wore an eyeglass, which stood him in good stead, since the number of persons he contrived *not* to see at one of his meets was truly remarkable. He also was distinguished by a stony stare very disconcerting to its object. His eyes always seemed to look just a little above his neighbour's head, making that individual feel there *must* be something wrong or queer about his hat.

Another famous M. A. was old General Prosieboy, or The Squasher, as he was lovingly called by his intimates. He was a most useful personage, and had derived his sobriquet from the fact that he could annihilate an objectionable stranger better than any other single M. A. in existence. His method was very simple. He discharged a volley of oaths at the offender, and as these were by no means choice, generally forcible, and nearly always un-provoked, nine times out of ten the audacious enemy who had dared to address an M. A. without waiting to be first spoken to by him, retired in dismay, and never repeated the hazardous experiment.

Once, and once only, it was said that The Squasher met his match. The gentle-man was fresh from California, and displayed a fluency, a facility and an originality of language, which fairly discomfited his opponent, whose vocabulary was limited in comparison.

Taking him all in all, Captain Straightem might fairly be reckoned the flower of the Mutual Adorationites. He was the best dressed, the coolest, the most silent, and least gregarious of the party. He had never been known to laugh, and seldom seen to smile. His brethen were loud in his praise. Of the whole dozen good fellows

who formed their ranks, he (always excepting themselves) was voted the best. As a
specimen of the right sort, he shone pre-
eminent.

He kept himself aloof, and never by any
chance fraternized with the vulgar herd.
As the owner of a large estate in the county,
he was a man of considerable position,
and looked up to accordingly, both by
those who had, and by those who had not,
the honour of his acquaintance.

And even his enemies respected him for
the brilliant way in which he rode to
hounds. They admitted that he had some
excuse for his extremely good opinion of
himself, but the other M. A.'s they declared
had none.

Still there was no doubt that the Mutual
Adorationites were on remarkably friendly
terms with No One. It must have been
the case, since nearly everybody else was
dubbed " a creature, a brute, or an out-

sider." Nobody was good enough for
them—at least, nobody under a baron.
Yet the singular part of the whole business
was this. If any one had told them that
their Hunt was not popular, and that they
were the sole cause of its unpopularity,
they would have received the statement
with a burst of incredulous indignation.
The truth was, they had not the faculty of
seeing things from any point of view but
their own. Hence the limitedness of their
vision.

CHAPTER II.

NECK OR NOTHING.

It would have deen difficult to conceive of a more melancholy day for the opening meet of the season than was Tuesday, the first of November, 188-.

When Captain Straightem's servant called his master about half-past eight o'clock, that gentleman turned in bed like a lazy porpoise rolling on the top of the water, yawned and murmured in a voice muffled by blankets: "What sort of a day is it, Dickinson?"

"A tremendously thick fog, sir," came the prompt reply, uttered in tones of unsympathetic cheerfulness. "You can't see twenty yards a'ead of you."

"The devil!" exclaimed Captain Straightem, wakening into sudden life, and springing out of bed, so as to ascertain for himself the exact state of the weather.

But to his disgust, on looking out of the window, he perceived at a glance that for once Dickinson had not exaggerated matters.

A dense fog lay over all the land, enshrouding both hills and valleys in its weird and ghostly embrace. It rested like a soft, grey sheet upon the fields, toning down to a sombre tint the bright green grass. As for the laurel hedges growing on either side of the drive, they were impregnated with moisture, and great wet drops rested on their glossy leaves.

Everything was dark, everything was dull, everything was damp.

He looked up at the sky, but could detect no break or gleam of light.

The prospects of the chase did not appear promising. Captain Straightem stifled an oath as he applied the razor to his clean-shaven face.

"Confounded bad luck! Still it may clear by-and-bye," he muttered, half-an-hour later on, when he sat down to his solitary breakfast in the big oak dining-room. And at any rate it won't do not to go to the meet."

But as the fog showed no signs of giving, he drew an armchair to the fire, toasted his toes, and read the newspaper, waiting and hoping that the weather would improve. It was late before he started, and even then, instead of galloping to covert as was his wont, he allowed his smart little hog-maned hack to proceed at a comparatively leisurely pace.

Consequently by the time he reached the place of meeting, the majority of the field had already assembled; but although it was now long past the advertised hour, Lord Littelbrane had not attempted to make a move.

As a matter of fact, it would not have been easy to hunt, since objects at a distance of only a few yards were almost undistinguishable. To ride to hounds if they ran fast—which they so frequently do on these mild damp days, when the heavy state of the atmosphere seems to prevent scent from rising and dispersing—would tax the powers of the keenest and most daring fox-hunter in existence.

"Deuced bore this d—d fog," growled his lordship, as soon as Captain Straightem joined the small and select circle which invariably gathered round him at the meet, as if to protect his noble person from any possible onslaught of the vulgar herd. "Deuced bore."

"Deuced," echoed Captain Straightem, laconically but sympathetically.

" 'Pon my soul, I hardly know what to do. Whether to take the hounds home or not. All these 'Arries,' " looking round contemptuously, " will feel terribly aggrieved if we don't show them some sort of sport on the first day of the season."

" Never mind them," put in General Prosieboy. " It's ourselves we've got to think of. Ourselves first, our horses second, our hounds third."

" What do you say to it, Straightem ? " asked Lord Littelbrane. For, as before explained, Captain Straightem was a feature of the Hunt, and his opinion went for a great deal.

" Well, if I were you, I should wait a bit longer before giving up. Folks don't like to be disappointed on these kind of occasions, and it's just on the cards that the weather may clear."

And sure enough it did, though at no time in a satisfactory manner.

But at twelve o'clock the sun struggled so gallantly with the fog, that for a few minutes he actually forced it to disperse before his pale radiance.

Loud were the congratulations, and universal the satisfaction, when Lord Littelbrane, without losing a moment, gave orders for the proceedings of the day to commence, and hounds were at once trotted off at a brisk pace, to draw a covert close by.

Half-an-hour elapsed, and sadness and despondency once more fell upon the spirits of the field ; for the improvement in the weather proved only temporary, and the heavy mist seemed to roll down worse than ever. Phœbus turned white and sickly like an ailing child, then sullenly hid his face.

"If this goes on we shall *have* to give it up, whether we like it or not," said Lord Littelbrane gloomily.

The words were scarcely out of his mouth before a loud "gane forrard aw-a-ay" proclaimed that Reynard had left the snug undergrowth of the covert. There was evidently a hot scent in the open, for the hounds dashed out after him, close at his brush, and almost directly were lost to vision, engulphed, as it were, by the enveloping fog.

They threw their tongues merrily, and could be heard, though not seen.

And now began a curious chase; for every man had to ride by ear instead of by eye, and he who was deaf stood but a sorry chance.

Foxes are famed for their subtilty; and this one, as if on purpose to baffle his pursuers, chose about as rough and awkward a route as he could have selected in the whole country.

Fences loomed dark and formidable, their dimensions increased instead of diminished by the imperfect light. It was simply impossible to tell what they were like, until you were close upon them.

Horses sniffed the damp air through their open nostrils, and discharged it with disgust. They looked round suspiciously at this grey and unrecognisable world, were nervous and timid, and distrusted the commonest object. A log of wood, a cow, a stone, filled them with apprehension. And all this time, borne on the vaporous atmosphere, rang out the eager, murderous notes of hounds celebrated for their slaying qualities.

They were positively racing ahead.

But alack! alack! How to keep up with them? The task seemed well nigh impossible, and each man realized to his bitter cost that there are some days in every season when hunting is attended with more pain than pleasure. Days when hounds, fences, elements defy you simultaneously. Five minutes sufficed to place the field in disorder. Their ranks opened and spread in every direction ; and dire was the confusion that resulted.

Only Burnett (the huntsman), Captain Straightem, and a couple of hard-riding farmers succeeded in getting well away. Their nerve and promptitude served them in good stead ; but they had to ride as they had never ridden in their lives before. It was a case of neck or nothing.

Friendly gates could not be taken advantage of, as usual ; for to-day the Pack would have vanished from view in the time that they took to open. The only chance of keeping with hounds was to keep close to their heels and negotiate every possible and impossible fence that came in the way. Providence must provide for the rest.

Crash, crash go the timbers of a stiff double oxer, as the gallant quartette fly it, each man charging a different place.

One of the farmers is down—no, his horse recovers himself. He staggers for a pace or two, then gallops on as before, fearful of losing his companions.

Suddenly is heard a shrill whistle.

It is the first intimation given to the pursuers that they are close to a railway.

"By God!" exclaims Burnett in agitated tones; "the hounds will be cut to pieces." For he knows by the sound that they are just ahead.

He calls them by name; first in commanding, then in entreating, finally in frantic language. Never has his horn given forth such loud and urgent blasts.

But their blood is up, and they heed him not.

In another second an express train dashes into their midst, and two of the best bitches in the whole Pack will never

go a-hunting again, or stretch their fleet
limbs over the broad pastures. Burnett is
in despair.

He wrings his hands like a woman, and
as he dismounts hastily and bends over the
mangled carcases of his dead darlings—
those hounds that were his pride and his
delight—the tears gather in his eyes, whilst
his honest, weather-beaten face twitches
with sorrow.

" Darn this fog," he exclaims resentfully.
" It ain't fit to hunt in."

But the companions of poor Milkmaid
and Merrylass evidently hold a different
opinion. With deadly zest and joyous
music they fling forward after their fox,
every murderous instinct awakened and
desiring gratification.

A solitary horseman is with them now,
and follows their bold career. Burnett has
stayed with his hounds, the fog has
swallowed up the two farmers, who, until

this point, have maintained their own right well.

On the face of him who smiles so rarely a solemn smile has settled. To have bested the field is the one delight of his life. He can conceive of no higher pleasure.

Swish! And he tears through a great, black bullfinch, and is almost dragged from his saddle. Slap! And the bough of an overhanging tree catches him one on the mouth.

His countenance brightens still more, though the blood is spurting from his lip. His pulses quicken and his eye dilates, for the dangers and the difficulties of this particular chase lend it a special charm. When he thinks it all over in his armchair after a good dinner, he will feel excusably triumphant and elated in proportion to the obstacles overcome.

But what is this black thing looming

through the fog? Oh, for a ray of sunshine !

It might be a fence, it might be a house, it might be anything, for all he can tell.

The pulsations of his heart grow loud. He can hear them beating against his ribs. But the hounds have already disappeared behind the mysterious barrier, and where they go he is determined to follow. Whatever this man's faults may be, he is brave and knows no fear.

Besides, he has beneath him one of the most perfect and resolute hunters that ever looked through a bridle. A hunter who has carried him four seasons, and hardly put a foot wrong.

Captain Straightem leans forward in the saddle, pats his good horse's neck and speaks an encouraging word to him. Then he steadies him a trifle, and just when he is about to take off gives him his head. The animal knows his business, and is as courageous as a lion.

He springs from his hind legs, and oh ! ! !

Ten minutes afterwards, when Burnett, Lord Littelbrane, and some half-dozen others, riding in search of the hounds, came to the fence in question they prudently avoided it; and went through a bridle-gate which they had the good fortune to espy, congratulating themselves on not being forced to jump such a regular man-trap.

And yet the nerves of most of them were inclined to be more shaken than if they had made the attempt. For an unexpected sight met their vision.

Hard by, lying there on the ground all by himself, some ten or twelve yards distant from the fence, was Captain Straightem.

His horse had galloped away, and could

nowhere be seen, though a track of red blood seemed to tell that he must have been badly hurt in his fall.

For the thin dark line of treacherous metal, which has been responsible for so many accidents in the hunting-field, was bent and twisted, and in parts tufts of fine chestnut-coloured hair adhered to the rusty wire.

Captain Straightem lay there quite still. He never moved or spoke when his companions crowded around him.

His face was turned upwards to the sodden sky, one hand was clenched, and held between its stiffened fingers a bunch of grass torn from its roots, and in his wide open eyes there rested a dull and vacant look, which somehow struck terror in the hearts of the bystanders.

It filled them with a nameless dread, a horrible suspicion, which, staring blankly into each other's sobered faces, they had, in the first startlingness of the shock, not courage to mention.

And the soft fog curled itself around the dark twigs of the hedge, and as a memento of its passage left hanging from each pointed thorn a trembling drop. Even in that short space of time it had silvered the fallen man's hair and covered with a white, humid covering his red coat, his snowy breeches, his top-boots, and all the brave insignia of the chase, with which only that morning he had sallied forth, full of life and spirits.

CHAPTER III.

THE MUTUAL ADORATIONITES SUSTAIN AN
IRREPARABLE LOSS.

LORD LITTELBRANE was the first to speak.

" I fear this is a bad business," he said huskily. " Does anyone know if there is a doctor out hunting to-day ? "

" Yes, I do, my lord," answered Burnett, touching his cap. " I saw Mr. Smith of Cottlebury at the meet, riding that there rat-tailed grey cob of his."

" Go and fetch him then this minute."

" Yes, my lord."

" And hark you, Burnett, don't spare your horse. For once in your life don't mind if you bring him back lame or not ;

only for God's sake find this Mr. Smith;
and get him to come here immediately."

It was not often that his lordship spoke at
such length or with so much energy and
decision.   Burnett at once realized the
gravity of the situation, and galloped off
at full speed in the direction from which he
had recently arrived.

When he had gone, Lord Littelbrane
knelt down on the damp grass by the side
of his prostrate friend, and putting out his
hand, placed it under Captain Straightem's
red coat, and over his heart. "I can't
feel it beat," he said tremulously, looking
up with troubled eyes, at those who stood
near. "It is horribly still, and there's a
look about his face which I don't half like.
Straightem, old boy," giving him a slight
shake, "pull yourself together."

But no answer was forthcoming.   Still
the same unnatural quietude prevailed.

And now the truth, in all its solemnity

and horror, began to force itself upon Lord
Littelbrane's comprehension. Fiercely and
feverishly he endeavoured to thrust it from
him, but the thought grew and grew, and
turned his blood to ice. He had seen too
many bad accidents in the hunting field
not to know what this portended. Only last
year a young rough rider of his own had
been killed whilst following the hounds.

There was the same expression on the
lad's face as on Captain Straightem's. He
recalled it with a shudder. His nerves had
been shaken then, but now he felt as if
they would give way altogether. He
seemed stunned and dazed by the magnitude of the disaster.

For this man, lying here so pale and
still, was his friend. He had not so many
that he could afford to lose his best one
—the only one really after his heart.
Captain Straightem was endeared to him
through many ties of association, such as

when youths grow up, bind them closely together. They had been born in the same county, and in the same year. As boys they had gone to the same school and displayed an equal amount of stupidity. As men, horses and hounds proved an unfailing bond of union between them. They knew each other's peculiarities, and their ideas of the position and importance of a Mutual Adorationite were identical.

And besides all this, Lord Littelbrane was not only proud of Captain Straightem, but he entertained a species of veneration cr him. There was not another man in all the Hunt who could ride like the gallant captain. If any serious misfortune had now happened to him, who could he— Lord Littelbrane—depend upon in future to uphold the honour of their sacred body, and show these rough-and-tumble fellows the real scientific way to cross a country?

And if—if things were as he feared, who

would jog home with him at his own peculiar pace, after a hard day's hunting, not taxing his conversational powers by an irritating flow of small talk, but only at long intervals giving vent to some choice and almost monosyllabic remark. Then, too, who would support him through thick and thin, in the various difficulties raised by covert-owners, farmers, poultry-losers, subscribers, &c.

A lump came into Lord Littelbrane's throat, which threatened to impede his respiration. He turned his head hastily away, so that none present should perceive the moisture which suddenly dimmed his eyes.

Meanwhile a couple of sheep hurdles had been torn up from a turnip field close by, and on these they laid Captain Straightem's body, after first raising it reverently from the ground.

Then the mournful little procession

marched slowly and sadly through the wet fields, until at length a road was reached. Near this road stood a tidy cottage, and in its parlour they deposited their burden on the sofa.

Lord Littelbrane would not leave his friend, even for a moment. He kept his eyes rivetted on Captain Straightem's face, in the hope of seeing some sign of life return to it. But one of the party kept watch outside the door, and paced restlessly up and down the road, waiting and longing for Doctor Smith's arrival.

So the minutes passed anxiously away. They seemed interminable, and the gloom of the atmosphere coincided with the gloom of their spirits.

For although they tried by every restorative they could think of, to bring colour to the fallen man's cheek, warmth to his flesh, and light to his eye, all their attempts proved vain.

At last the sound of hoofs was heard, and in another second, Burnett emerged like a giant from the fog, followed by Doctor Smith on his grey cob. Both horses were panting, and gave evidence of the speed at which they had travelled.

The doctor dismounted, and after a few words of explanation from Lord Littelbrane, who came out to greet him, flung the reins to Burnett, and disappeared within the cottage. Arrived there, one look was enough to convince him that here were no bones to set, no cuts to strap, or wounds to dress.

Captain Straightem was past the aid of man. Not all the skill and science in the world could avail him now. He had gone where such things were unable to penetrate.

Doctor Smith shook his head, and his countenance assumed an unusually grave expression.

"Well!" asked Lord Littelbrane in an awestruck voice, for he knew what was coming.

"Is there—is there any chance of his getting over it?"

"Not in this world," said the doctor seriously. "Captain Straightem is dead, and has been so for some time."

"Dead!" exclaimed the other with sharp anguish. "Oh! no, not dead, surely not dead. I will telegraph to London for the best advice. Somebody *must* pull him through,"

"Neither I, nor anybody else, can do him any good, poor fellow! I only wish that we could."

At this terrible confirmation of his worst fears, Lord Littelbrane sank down on his knees by Captain Straightem's side, and buried his face in his hands.

Absolute silence prevailed throughout the room. None felt inclined to break it.

Only every now and again could be heard a suppressed sob, which escaped from his lordship almost involuntarily.

In spite of his vapidity, his reserve, and curious conceit he had a heart. During many years he had striven to conceal its existence, but now it burst through that veneer of impenetrability, on which, as a Mutual Adorationite, he had long prided himself.

Something seemed to give way within him, and he bowed his head and wept like a child.

The effort to maintain a dignified stoicism was beyond his strength.

And those who had never liked him— who had called him a fool, a prig, an aristocrat—thought better of him at this moment than they had ever done. The resentment of years vanished. The slights and insults of seasons were forgotten. For the first time almost in their lives, they felt that he was human: a creature like themselves, who loved, and mourned, and suffered. "He ain't such a bad chap after all!" they murmured to one another. "It's his way and very likely he don't mean anything by it. We have been foolish enough to take offence where probably none was intended."

Meantime Dr. Smith was making a minute examination in order to ascertain the exact cause of death. As a hunting man himself, he felt an unusual interest in the case. He soon discovered what had happened.

"Poor chap," he said, in his rough but sympathetic way. (At any other time Lord Littelbrane would have winced at hearing his best friend called a " poor chap," but he was too thoroughly upset and startled out of his usual groove to take any notice now.) "He has broken his neck. It is quite clear to my mind, that when he fell he landed on the point of his chin, which caused the entire head to be violently jerked backwards, from which dislocation of the cervical vertebræ ensued." Then he looked commiseratingly at Lord Littelbrane, and added :

" Don't take on so, my lord. This is a dreadful business, but it should at least be some consolation to you to know that death was instantaneous, and that your friend was spared all pain."

But Lord Littelbrane shook his sleek, fair head, and refused to be comforted.

The shock was so great and so entirely unexpected, that for once in his life it made him forget himself and his dignity. Later on it would be a cause of shame, when he reflected that he had allowed these " outsiders " to see that he possessed feelings and emotions, and was not the iceberg he strove to appear.

But the " outsiders " respected his grief

and, as before stated, thought none the worse of him in consequence.

While all this was going on, a considerable crowd had collected round the cottage.

Ill news travels apace, as the saying tells us, and stragglers began to pour in from all sides.

"What, dead? Straightem dead? You don't mean it!"

"Yes, I do though. Terrible thing. Been dead an hour. Had a bad fall and broke his neck."

"Dear me! How dreadful! How did it happen?"

"The old story. Wire. Farmer deserves to be strung up."

The above were a specimen of the remarks that went the round. Everybody looked shocked and saddened. For even those who had not known Captain Straightem personally, knew him by sight, and were sobered by the intelligence of the disaster that had befallen him.

Men fear death; and none so much as the strong and healthy, whose minds refuse to dwell on the possibility of annihilation, and whose physical vitality laughs it to scorn. But this sudden cutting off of one of their number brought home, in a forcible way, the dangers of hunting.

What had happened to Captain Straightem might have happened equally to themselves. They—not he—might have been lying dead inside the homely cottage.

The mere idea was enough to shake their nerves, and to send a cold shudder down their spines. Sadly and quietly they gradually dispersed, whilst Burnett collected his hounds—only twenty-one couple now, instead of twenty-two—and moved slowly off in the direction of the kennels. His orders were, that they should not come out again for a fortnight. There was to be no hunting in the Morbey Anstead country during that time.

If Lord Littelbrane could do nothing else, he was determined to pay respect to the dead man's memory.

And so ended the first day of the season. It had both begun and finished badly, and the Mutual Adorationites had received a blow which quite prostrated them. For their king was no more, and they knew of none to fill his place. Where was the man who could combine such brilliant horsemanship with such hauteur, such exclusiveness and reserve?

CHAPTER IV.

LORD LITTELBRANE FEELS LONELY.

A WEEK after the sad event recorded in the last chapter, Lord Littelbrane and General Prosieboy sat down to a *tête-à-tête* dinner at the house of the former.

His lordship was a bachelor, and not much given to running after the fair sex.

As a matter of fact, few of the Mutual Adorationites were married men. Mutual adoration did not seem to work well in the bosom of one's family. Not many wives admired and looked up to their husbands as they ought. They had a nasty knack of bringing their lords and masters' weak points to light. So said the M. A.'s. Anyhow they did not approve of matrimony

as an institution. It broke up their ranks,
and introduced an altogether new and un-
welcome element. Once a man married he
was never quite the same. He was no
longer allowed to follow his own judgment, and his visiting list soon showed a
sad deterioration.

For this, and many other reasons, it
resulted that if one of the genuine Mutual
Adorationites was rash enough to turn
Benedict-he was generally treated with a
considerable amount of frigidity for a very
long time afterwards.

It took several years before the offence
was forgiven, and even if the bride were
altogether charming she never found herself wholly accepted. The M. A.'s, to one
man, felt that they owed her a grudge, for
weakening dear Adolphus's or dear Sidney's
allegiance to their sacred body. But as
regards Lord Littelbrane, he could not help
entertaining an uneasy conviction that

some day or other he was bound to get married. An heir to the title was imperative. He had told himself this for the last ten or twelve years, during which he made sundry virtuous resolutions, and repeatedly determined to sacrifice his bachelor independence ; but so far these good resolves had come to nothing.

He would be forty-six next birthday, and Littelbrane Castle was still without a mistress. Match-making mammas, possessing ambitious daughters, had angled for him in vain, and now, in despair, they had given him up as a bad job, and reluctantly turned their attention elsewhere. Both the late Captain Straightem and his lordship seemed equally proof against feminine blandishments, and it was rumoured in the county that they would never take a wife to weaken, if not destroy their intimacy, and prevent them from being constantly together.

But since his friend's sudden death, Lord Littelbrane's whole mental condition had undergone a complete alteration. Circumstances had brought about a curious change in his ideas. When he looked round at his great big barrack of a house, with its endless rooms, swarms of servants, and absence of any real comfort, it struck him all at once that he was very lonely, that many a labouring man, with a stout red-cheeked wife and half a dozen babies, was happier far than he. He began to wonder what it would feel like to be the father of a family, to set his little children on his knee, and play with their golden curls. A strange yearning came over him for sympathy and companionship—a sympathy and companionship even closer than that which he had just lost.

And thus wondering and speculating, his thoughts reverted to a certain Lady De Fochsey, who was both young and pretty, and the widow of a deceased baronet. She was a very smart, natty little lady, who in her scarlet jacket and white waistcoat, did credit to his Hunt. The Mutual Adorationites all knew her, and on account of her good looks, received her as one of themselves. True he had never paid her any attention, but that might easily be rectified, and he fancied she would accept his advances graciously.

Still, it was a desperate plunge, this which he contemplated taking—so desperate that nothing but the loss of his friend could have made him entertain the idea in earnest.

His first notion was to invite Lady De Fochsey to come and take a quiet little dinner with him, explaining that he felt very melancholy and required cheerful society. He was convinced she was cheerful. Her laugh rang out so merrily at the covert side that it had once or twice

actually aroused his curiosity as to the
cause of her mirth. Women ought to be
cheerful. He liked them so, as long as
they were not " loud." He hoped she was
not " loud," and wished he knew her well
enough to make quite sure.

But when he came to consider the
slightness of his acquaintanceship with
Lady De Fochsey, he arrived at the conclusion that it was out of the question for
him to ask her to dinner in this sudden and
informal manner. So, as his solitude was
rapidly becoming unbearable, he invited old
General Prosieboy instead, who although
he did not much appreciate the Castle
cuisine, liked being able to say: " Oh, ah !
my dear fellow ! If you've nothing better
to do to-night, come and take pot-luck
with me. Damme though, I forgot, I'm
dining with Lord Littelbrane. See you
some other time I hope." But he always
took good care to leave that " other time "

indefinite, and never alluded to it when next he met the "dear fellow." The dining room at Littelbrane Castle was very large and also very cold. No matter how big the fire, it only warmed one portion of the apartment. The old windows rattled, the old doors creaked, and the wind seemed to blow in at all sorts of possible and impossible places.

Round and round the dinner-table stalked a pompous, grey-haired butler and a couple of solemnly-stupid footmen. These worthies took special care to prevent their master and his guest from indulging too freely in the pleasures of the table.

The soup might have been a liquid medicine, to be taken cautiously—one to two table-spoons in a little water. The fish was served out in such lilliputian quantities, that it was only an aggravation to a hungry, healthy man. The entrée consisted of a tiny oyster patty apiece, with

4*

one single oyster in its midst—that is for the eaters. There were plenty of patties on the dish, but they were smuggled away with a sleight-of-hand that would have reflected credit upon Messrs. Maskelyne and Cooke. This was the more provoking as General Prosieboy was fond of oysters.

Mutton ? Yes ! there was mutton certainly, but what was the good of that when you were helped to a slice that might have been carved from the breast of a lark.

And yet, night after night, Lord Littelbrane sat down to this mockery of a meal because he considered it to be " the thing ! " He would rather go without a morsel and be waited upon by three pompous menservants, than he would dispense with their services, and help himself *as* he liked, and *how* he liked.

So much for fashion.

But General Prosieboy was not exactly a

fashionable man, and moreover he possessed a remarkably good appetite.

At home he invariably insisted on his
parlour-maid putting each separate dish
on the table. Then he *did* get something
to eat. But really! at Littelbrane Castle,
in spite of all the fine furniture, old armour,
and retinue of servants, when he got up
from the table he felt very nearly if not
quite as hungry as when he sat down
to it.

However, he was on his company
manners, and stood too much in awe of
Lord Littelbrane's exalted rank—his father
had made all his money in Prosieboy's
antibilious pills—to air his sentiments
aloud. Had he done so they would probably have been translated by oaths. On
the present occasion, with a mighty effort
of self-control, he succeeded in maintaining
a decorous silence, mentally determining to
have up that excellent piece of cold beef

he had had for luncheon, directly he reached home.

He fumed inwardly all the time the three great, silent sentinels were in the room, but when they removed their restraining presence, carrying everything eatable away with them that they could, the atmosphere seemed suddenly to have grown less oppressive. Then the two gentlemen drew up their chairs close to the fire-side, and placed the port and claret on the mantel-piece where it was easily get-at-able.

After consuming four or five glasses, the strings of their tongues gradually became unloosened. The Littelbrane wine was good, and General Prosieboy revenged himself upon *it*, for not having dined.

"Ahem!" he said communicatively, and with the air of a man who considers he is imparting a wonderful piece of intelligence. "I forgot to tell you before, but I've seen him."

His lordship at that moment was thinking quite sentimentally — thanks to the Château Lafitte—of Lady De Fochsey's rosy, smiling face, her trim figure and sparkling blue eyes.

"Eh! what! Seen him? Seen who?" he asked with rather a guilty start.

"Why, the new man. The man who comes in for all poor old Straightem's property. The nephew, in short."

"Have you, by Jove! And what's he like? Can we have anything to do with him?" And as he made the inquiry, Lord Littelbrane's countenance assumed an expression which seemed to say that he, for one, was convinced the Mutual Adoration-ites could *not* be hand in glove with a total stranger, hailing from the colonies.

"Impossible," said General Prosieboy emphatically.

His lordship gave a sigh of relief.

"Why?" he asked, subsiding into his

usual languid state, which forcibly suggested a torpid liver.

"Because, as far as I can judge, he's the
wrong sort altogether."

"Ah! I expected so, and should have
been very much astonished had he proved
anything else."

"It seems he has lived all his life in
Australia, and has never been to England
before. In fact, one could almost tell as
much from looking at him. Colonist is
stamped upon him from the crown of his
hat to the sole of his boots."

"Poor devil!" exclaimed Lord Littelbrane commiseratingly.

"Did Captain Straightem never mention
this bushman of a relative?" asked the
General, with an elderly man's curiosity.
"I don't seem to have heard of him."

"Oh! yes, lots of times. But never
without a shudder. Poor Harry was so
refined," sighing heavily. "He told me,

only the morning of his death, that the fellow had arrived unexpectedly and proposed running down to Straightem Court to pay him a visit. 'Awful bore,' said Harry, 'and the worst of it is, I don't know how the deuce to put him off. He's got a sort of right to come, since, unless I marry and have children, he's the next heir to the property.' "

" He has acquired a most unfortunate right to it now," said General Prosieboy lugubriously.

" Yes, worse luck. Times are indeed sadly changed. I wonder though if I ought to be civil to the man on Harry's account?" And Lord Littelbrane looked uneasily at his companion.

" I really don't see any necessity for it. It does your Lordship's heart immense credit even to have suggested such a thing ; but, I assure you, you can't possibly associate with this aborigine. If you had only seen the creature as I saw him to-day, at the railway station, dressed in a brown velveteen suit, with a flaring red tie, and a pair of checked trousers that reminded one of a chess-board, you would have recognised, in spite of your natural kindness, that it is quite out of the question for a man in your position and of your rank to notice so very peculiar a person. Why, damme! he wears clothes that are enough in themselves to make anybody who has the remotest notion of what is customary in civilized society cut him on the spot."

"And there is such a lot in clothes," murmured his lordship. "I think it was Kingsley who said, you can transform any gentleman into a blackguard—at least as far as outward appearances go—by simply taking away his white collar and substituting a coloured scarf in its stead. By-the-bye, what is the duffer's name? It's not

Straightem, I know, thank God for that?"

"No, it's Jarrett—Robert P. Jarrett—I saw it painted on his portmanteau."

"I wonder if Mr. Robert P. Jarrett means to favour us with his presence out hunting."

"I expect he is sure to," returned the General. "These Australians mostly take kindly to sport."

"Confound the fellow! We shall have him jumping on my hounds, and making that an excuse to scrape acquaintance with me. Really Prosieboy, if he turns out objectionable, as I fully expect from your description of him, you must come to the rescue."

"With all my heart, my Lord," replied his companion, dilating his nostrils, and sniffing the air like an old war-horse who smells powder and is eager to begin the fray. "You leave Mr. Robert P.

Jarrett to me. I'll soon settle him, never fear."

"That's all right. Remember Prosieboy, I count upon you should any emergency arise."

And with these words, Lord Littelbrane dismissed the subject.

A long silence succeeded, during which host and guest lit a couple of cigars and smoked away steadily. The occupation evidently strained every faculty ; for conversation languished, both feeling that after their recent outburst of eloquence they needed time to recruit their forces.

General Prosieboy was the first to make a remark. It was scarcely as original as might have been expected from the long period of incubation required to give it birth.

"Feels cold to-night," he said. "I think we shall have a frost."

"Oh! Ah! very likely. Time of year

we may expect them," answered his lordship.

Another silence of five minutes followed
this brilliant sally.

Then the General again gave vent to an
oracular utterance :

" Shouldn't wonder if we had snow before
long."

" No, nor I."   .   .   .   .

Whereupon they both puffed away at
their cigars harder than ever.

Their ideas appeared totally exhausted.
Even the weather failed to furnish a further
supply.

But by-and-bye a large lump of coal fell
down on the grate with a clatter.   Lord
Littelbrane seized the tongs, and stooped
to pick it up.   This broke the spell.

" Awful bore when coals tumble about,"
he said.

" Awful," replied General Prosieboy.

Puff, puff, puff.   Apparently neither of

them could think of anything more to say. The General could only talk when he was drunk or in a rage. Take away his oaths and his liquor and he was nowhere. As for Lord Littelbrane he never could understand why when people dine together they should be supposed to keep up a perpetual chatter. What was the pleasure of it in comparison with the fatigue?

Eleven o'clock strikes, and General Prosieboy rises from his seat, and throws away the end of his cigar.

"Think I must be going home," he says.

"Must you?" rejoins Lord Littelbrane passively. He never presses his guests to stay after half-past ten. In the hunting season he invariably keeps early hours.

"Yes, think so. Good night, my lord. Hope you will cheer up before long."

General Prosieboy's hand is on the handle of the door as he speaks. In another moment he would have vanished into the corridor.

His lordship plucked up all his courage, and made a desperate effort.

"By the way," he said, whilst a flush rose to his sallow face, "what's your opinion of that little Lady De Fochsey? She's the right sort, ain't she?"

The question took General Prosieboy completely by surprise, but he was far too diplomatic a gentleman to express the astonishment that he felt.

"Oh, yes!" he answered in an off-hand way, seeing he was evidently desired to express approval. "Quite the right sort; a very nice little woman indeed. I know nothing whatever against her, except that she's rather too thick with some of the outsiders."

"Ah! she's young. She'll soon learn to distinguish, especially with the advantage of a little judicious guidance. But I'm

keeping you standing ; good night, Prosieboy, good night."

And so saying, Lord Littelbrane shook
hands with his guest, and saw him out at
the hall door. But this last remark of his
host's had given the General much food for
reflection.

No sooner was he fairly seated within the
sheltering walls of his one-horse fly, than
he drew a long breath of dismay.

"Thunder and lightning!" he exclaimed
dejectedly. " So that's the little game, is
it ? Why! bless my heart alive, I do
believe he's thinking of getting married.
Was there ever such a set-out? There
won't be one of us left at this rate. First
a death, then a marriage ! Upon my soul,
I hardly know which is the worst of the
two. As for the Hunt, it's going to
the dogs altogether ; and if Lord Littelbrane don't look out, he'll be having his
country over-run with strangers, and a

lot of confounded radicals who not only believe in but *act* on the principle of one man being as good as another. Such rot indeed!" he wound up indignantly.

His heart was so heavy within him at the mere thought of Lord Littelbrane's contemplating matrimony, that when he got home he found the cold beef insufficient to comfort the sinkings of his inner man. He was forced to take a very stiff tumbler of brandy and water in addition.

"Just to quiet the system, Mary, my dear; just to quiet the system," he explained to his pretty parlour-maid (he never would have an ugly servant in his house), chucking her familiarly under the chin.

"Hexactly, sir; I understands."

"The fact of the matter is, Mary, I've received a shock, and it has knocked me all of a heap."

"Take another glass of brandy, sir. It's uncommon soothing to the nerves."

"Yes, Mary, I will. I think your suggestion is a wise one."

He found it so wise that it was close upon one o'clock before he could at length be induced to toddle off to his bed. Mary had to help him to get there ; but once safely between the sheets, thanks to the joint effect of Lord Littelbrane's port and of his own three-star Henessey, he slept the sleep of the just.

He had effectually soothed his nerves by addling his wits.

CHAPTER V.

A STRANGER IN THE LAND.

Robert Jarrett's mother and the late Captain Straightem had been only brother and sister.

As children, the boy and girl were devoted to each other, but when they grew up, fate, that capricious goddess, cast their lots in very different places.

The young man went into the Guards, looked brave and handsome in his uniform, spent a considerable amount of money, idled away his days, denied himself no luxury, and, as times go, was a credit to his doting father.

As for Fanny, well, poor Fanny made what was considered a most terrible

5*

"mésalliance." She was destined to marry into the aristocracy and she married an agriculturist.

When this unfortunate event took place she was very young; only a month over seventeen, and had but just returned from a fashionable boarding school in Brighton, where she had been finishing her education previous to making her entry into society.

But, alas! like a silly romantic child, she fell desperately in love with a young man, aged twenty-one, who had been sent down to Stiffshire to learn farming; presumably because he had not brains enough to learn anything else, or to pass the necessary examinations for the army. At any rate, he took to turnips and oil-cake.

He was a gentleman by birth, and that was about all that could be said for him—at least, so Squire Straightem declared, when his daughter came with tears in her pretty, blue eyes, and begged him to give his consent to her engagement with Mr. Charles Jarrett.

The squire turned purple in the face, almost had a fit of apoplexy, and refused flatly. The idea! Why, the girl must be mad.

But Fanny was too much smitten by her lover's pleasant manners, and professions of affection, to listen to reason. She even thought there was something fine in making a sacrifice for the sake of him she loved. Anyhow, she was young, ignorant and headstrong.

Her grandmother had left her five thousand pounds. Over this sum she possessed absolute control. Master Charles' income consisted of two hundred a year. He was an orphan, and had neither expectations nor interest; but, to do him justice, he was genuinely attached to Fanny. To make a long story short, one fine day the imprudent and impatient young couple got married secretly, trusting that when they were actually man and wife the squire would relent and be induced to make them some further provision than that derived from their own very limited means.

But, like many others, they reckoned without their host.

Old Squire Straightem flew into a towering passion when he found that little, innocent, blue-eyed Fanny had defied him by taking the law into her own hands. Refusing to listen to her prayers for forgiveness, he swore a mighty oath that she should never set foot inside his house again. And he was as good as his word.

Mr. and Mrs. Charles Jarrett were therefore obliged to fall back upon their own resources. These, as we know, were not large. Fanny was inexperienced; she had been extravagantly brought up, and had no notion of housekeeping.

For six months they tried living in England; but they found that, do what they would, they were running into debt. No one could have had better intentions than the poor little bride, but she had everything to learn in her new life, and also a good deal to unlearn. It came hardly to her at first, and nobody need blame her if she made a few blunders. Most of us similarly situated would have done the same.

But they were a brave young couple, and when things seemed likely to go from bad to worse, they made up their minds to shake themselves free of the old shackles and start afresh in Australia. This they did; and with Fanny's five thousand pounds Charles Jarrett bought a sheep farm and stocked it with sheep.

Sometimes they had good years, sometimes they had bad; but they managed to keep their heads above water, and on the whole prospered fairly well. At all events Fanny never regretted the step she had taken, even although it had completely estranged her from her father and brother.

Charles Jarrett was far too easy-going and indolent a man to grow rich. A large family—of whom Robert was the eldest— and as the years went by, very indifferent health, effectually prevented him from making a fortune.

Thus, when he died at the comparatively early age of forty-eight, he was unable to do more than leave his wife and children above want.

But Robert, or Bob as he was familiarly called, had already shown himself to be a far more active, energetic and stirring individual than his father. He had not inherited Charles Jarrett's constitutional laziness of disposition, which had effectually prevented him from getting on in the world.

The farm was left to Robert. The young man soon discovered that to a great extent it had been grievously mismanaged, and that its powers of production had never really been tested. His first care was to put everything in thorough order.

Next he tried hard to improve the breed of sheep and introduced several new strains of blood. But he was not satisfied with those that were available; and after a couple of years scraped enough money together to provide for the family in his absence, and to take him to England.

Naturally, he was eager to visit the country where his mother had been born and bred. He was aware that, as matters stood at present, Captain Straightem's property would revert to him. But he never counted on this contingency.

It seemed altogether too remote, for Captain Straightem was by no means an old man, and might at any time take it into his head to get married.

Bob, in his own mind, was so convinced that sooner or later his uncle would espouse a better-half, that it very rarely occurred to him to think of himself as only one step removed from a magnificent estate and close upon fifteen thousand a year.

No such thought actuated him when he set foot upon English ground and deemed it his duty to write and inform Captain Straightem of his arrival, in case that gentleman might express a wish to make his (Bob's) acquaintance.

To this letter he had received no reply; in lieu thereof came a lawyer's communication, formally worded, acquainting him of the fact, that owing to his uncle's sudden decease in the hunting field, he was now the possessor of Straightem Court, with all its adjoining lands. Bob's amazement may be more easily conceived than described.

In fact his astonishment was too great to allow him to derive any immediate satisfaction from the extraordinary alteration that had taken place in his prospects.

It did just flash through his mind that henceforth, if he chose, he might apply his energies to improving the breed of English rather than of Australian sheep, but that was all.

It never even struck him that his presence might be necessary at Straightem Court, until he received a second letter from the family solicitor, requesting his immediate attendance. Then by slow degrees he began to realize that he, who was accustomed to rise with the sun, to saddle and dress his own horse, to be content with the coarse fare and to put his hand to every job that came in the way, was now transformed into a fine gentleman, who had nothing to do but take his pleasure and amuse himself from

morning till night. This dawned upon Bob
as such a stupendous idea that it almost
took away his breath. It is not an easy
thing when all your thoughts have been
attuned to a particular groove, suddenly to
divert them into another and totally un-
familiar one. It takes a little time before
the adaptation becomes complete.

Bob was a young man who possessed an
immense amount of vitality and of that
nervous force which delights in work and
in conquering it. He liked the active, even
if somewhat rough, life which he had
hitherto led.

He enjoyed the responsibility of being
the head of the family and of feeling that
his brothers and sisters were dependent on
him. It sent a thrill of pleasurable pride
through his frame to see their bright and
happy faces as they came clustering round
him after a hard day's work. Somehow or
other the simple homely way in which they

lived seemed to bind every member of the family, from the eldest to the youngest, in ties of close affection.

True they were not rich, each one had to take his or her share in the daily toil, but for all that they had been very, very happy.

Would they be as happy if they lived in a grand house, had any amount of money to spend and lots of servants to wait upon them, instead of waiting upon themselves as they had hitherto been accustomed to do?

Bob hoped so; but he was not quite sure.

This sudden change in their lives seemed to him a bit of an experiment; it might or it might not turn out well.

He was Australian born and bred, and loved the sunny land of his birth; he possessed a sturdy independence and manly bluntness, which did very well for the

colonies, but he was sensitive enough to feel
that, in his new position, his manners would
probably require a considerable amount of
toning down. In Australia people did not
wrap their speech up in silver paper, they
said what they meant and did not sneer at
conversation which owed its birth to home
interests, and often to home interests alone.

But Bob had not been four and twenty
hours in the old country before he realized
that a subtle difference existed between it
and the new; the former was more polished
if not so fresh; more fastidious and critical,
though infinitely less light-hearted.

Even as regarded his dress, he soon came
to have considerable misgivings.

His brown velveteen suit, red tie, and
checked trousers, no longer afforded him
quite the same satisfaction as on board ship.

Somehow they seemed out of place in
the London streets, where he noticed people
all dressed quietly and mostly in black or

dark colours. Once or twice his appearance evidently excited surprise, and he felt extremely uncomfortable, not knowing exactly what there was about it that was wrong.

In fact, if General Prosieboy had but known with how much inward trepidation " The Duffer, The Brute, The Creature " was about to enter into his kingdom, even he might have felt mollified and not been quite so hostilely inclined towards Captain Straightem's unknown nephew and successor.

But the die was cast; the fiat had gone forth.

Robert P. Jarrett was doomed beforehand.

The Mutual Adorationites had decided that he should neither be known nor yet visited.

Other people might take up with him if they chose; but *they* would not demean themselves by having anything whatever to do with an individual who wore the wrong kind of clothes, and had no pretensions of " the right sort."

Mr. Jarrett should be made to feel in every possible way that his presence in the county was undesired and superfluous; that he was unpardonably occupying a house which, but for him, might have been inhabited by a good fellow; and that under no circumstances could he ever be accepted as fit company for the Mutual Adorationites. If he insisted on coming out hunting, of course they could not actually prevent him. He had a right to gallop over the fields and tear after the hounds if he chose.

But nobody need speak to him, except to swear roundly at him if he got in the way, or committed the smallest error of inexperience.

They could all stare at him blankly, and

refuse to recognize his presence as a fellow-creature. They could feign deafness if he hazarded a remark; blindness if he came across their path.

They could show him the cold shoulder to his face, and abuse him to their heart's content behind his back.

And this the Mutual Adorationites, according to their usual manners and customs, were determined to do.

He should be snubbed, and snubbed effectively.

For had not General Prosieboy given out that their poor old friend Straightem's successor was a "duffer" and an "outsider," with whom they ought not to associate? And would it not be showing disrespect to the dead man's memory, if they received with open arms a nephew of whom, in his lifetime, he was evidently ashamed?

Yes. There was such a thing as *esprit*

de corps. If the Mutual Adorationites did not wish to be swamped altogether by the odious radical wave of the century, they were bound to uphold their ancient habits and customs.

Moreover, *they* were perfectly satisfied with themselves as they were, and wanted no innovations introduced amongst their ranks.

CHAPTER VI.

OPPRESSED BY SO MUCH GRANDEUR.

ALTHOUGH our friend Bob had heard and read a good deal of the luxurious and, to a great extent, indolent way in which English gentlemen live when at all well off, he had no really definite notions on the subject until he arrived at Straightem Court. His mother had often talked to her children of the magnitude of her old home ; but then seeing a thing with one's own eyes is very different from having an impression made upon your mind through the medium of somebody else's optics.

The number and size of the rooms at Straightem Court fairly amazed Bob.

" What are they all for ?   What are they

6*

all for?" he kept on asking of the family solicitor who showed him over the premises, and had promised to remain for a day or two.

"For use, I suppose," replied that worthy, with a strong accent of reproof.

"For use! Do you mean to tell me that one parlour is not enough for anybody? Why, on my farm in Australia, we never dreamt of wanting a dining, drawing, breakfast, billiard and reading room, as you seem to have here. And what's more, it ain't comfort—leastways, to my mind," concluded Bob, decidedly.

His companion looked at him with a smile half supercilious, half contemptuous.

"You'll soon get to alter some of your opinions, Mr. Jarrett. It is quite evident that you have lived very much out of the world."

"Damn his impudence," muttered Bob, *sotto voce.* "He talks as if there were no

other country but his own particular, little
sea-girt island. It's wonderful how ignorant
and how cheeky these Englishmen are.
There's no getting them to see themselves
in their true light."

But he kept his reflections to himself,
and turning sharply to his uncle's solicitor,
said :

"And pray, what about the servants?
Am I supposed to keep all this troop of
idle people, eating me out of house and
home? Because it strikes me that would
come uncommon rough on a fellow,
especially when, like myself, he is a
stranger at the game."

"You will be able to arrange all these
matters to your own satisfaction when once
you have regularly entered into possession,"
said the other stiffly, beginning to think
what a terrible, sharp, fresh, outspoken
aborigine this was.

"Come! that's a mercy at any rate,"

said Bob, with a sigh of relief; for the mere contemplation of maintaining so large a staff of domestics was oppressive, and filled him with dismay. Yet, distrustful of his own opinions on subjects of which hitherto he had had no experience, he added seriously: "Listen, Tomlinson. You are a sensible man, and can give me a straightforward answer to a straightforward question. I only want to get at the *reason* of things, and no doubt you can tell me what is the use of all these idle folks? It seems to me there are too many of them by half, and they only make work for one another."

Mr. Tomlinson scratched his head, and looked somewhat perplexed. The question put thus, was not altogether easy to answer.

"It is customary, Mr. Jarrett, in all large houses, to keep up a good establishment— that is to say, where there are sufficient means."

Bob's face assumed a thoughtful expression.

" I don't see," he said, "how one person, living quite alone like my late uncle, could possibly need so many people to minister to his wants. It seems an anomaly for a single man to employ such a number of servants just to attend to his mere personal requirements. Now, if *I* were an English gentleman, I should hate to feel myself dependent upon my cook, butler, or footman, as the case might be. It's turning a fellow into a regular slave, and a slave of a very poor, contemptible order."

" I suppose you learnt those ideas out in Australia," said Mr. Tomlinson rather uncomfortably, and on that account trying to infuse an extra amount of satire into his voice.

" Perhaps I did, and perhaps I didn't," answered Bob, a bit nettled by the solicitor's overbearing manner. " Anyhow, whether I learnt them in Australia or elsewhere, they are ideas of which I do not feel at all ashamed, and on the contrary should despise myself if I did not entertain. There is a padded person in this house, with sham white hair, and sham round calves, who comes to opon the door. Can you tell me what that cumbrous mass of human flesh, with its painful deficiency of human brains, is good for?—since I am convinced he has never done a stroke of real, honest work in his life. I ask this because the individual in question has aroused my curiosity."

"I presume you mean Charles, the footman. A very fine, well-made man, over six feet in height, and an ornament to any gentleman's establishment," returned Mr. Tomlinson.

"Ha, ha!" laughed Bob. "Just as a fatted ox is an ornament to the gentleman's farm. I begin to see matters in a clearer

light. Show evidently comes before use
over here."

" Charles answers the bells, waits at
table, and, as far as I know, has always
proved himself to be an honest and respect-
able servant," said Tomlinson, testily.

" My dear sir, honesty and respectability
are very excellent things in their way.
Nobody has a greater respect for them
than myself. But when you find these
admirable qualities united to intense slow-
ness of perception and pomposity of movement, to crass stupidity and the sloth of an
overfed pig, then you can't help thinking
that they are not all-sufficient. Now, last
night I wanted a glass of whisky and
water. At home I could have gone to the
cupboard, fetched the whisky bottle, boiled
myself a drop of water in the kettle, and
got what I wished for without further
trouble and little or no delay. Here, there
are a butler and a footman, therefore I rang

the bell. They either *did* not, or *would* not hear it. In about five minutes' time, after pulling frantically at the bell-rope till at last it gave way, my friend Charles appears. I explain my requirements. He disappears. I wait another ten minutes. Presumably the water is being boiled. Unluckily there is no longer any bell to pull. I wait impatiently, and try to smother the oaths that insist on rising to my lips. Presently I hear a leviathan tread—the tread of an elephant—sounding down the passage. With the deliberation with which all his movements are attended, Charles brings into the room a hot water jug. There is neither glass, whisky, nor sugar. I ask him where they are. He answers that he has forgotten, but will bring them in a minute. A minute, indeed! Exactly a quarter of an hour has elapsed since I first made known my modest demand. By this time, all my desire for a glass of comforting liquor has vanished. I resolve to do without it. No doubt I am all the better for my abstention, but it's no use telling me that this sort of thing is real comfort. It's downright bondage and nothing more, and comes from your old habits, your old institutions and your old country."

Mr. Tomlinson drew himself up to his full height, mentally classifying Bob as an unbearable Yahoo.

"I am sorry our manners and customs should appear so inferior to your Australian ones," he said, with an ill-disguised sneer.

"It's not that," Bob explained eagerly. "Only you don't seem to value Time in the way we do. Now, to waste a quarter of an hour over a drop of whisky would appear to us almost a sin; and not only a sin, but downright ridiculous into the bargain. But then, we are used to waiting upon ourselves, which no boubt makes all the difference."

"We English are a conservative race, I'll admit," returned Mr. Tomlinson, in a more conciliatory tone; "but it is rather hard to find one's own children turn round and abuse one."

"My dear sir," exclaimed Bob, pray don't imagine for a single moment that I have not the greatest respect and admiration for your race. Why! what have I come over here for, except to pick up a few wrinkles, and profit by some of your insular notions But you must forgive me if, in my blundering way, I try to distinguish where you are ahead of us, and where we are ahead of you. We look up to old England with intense veneration, but then, even the best of mothers gets ancient, and leaves her offspring with an advantage of youth on their side. There are too many of you over here. Your population increases, and you are bound in by the sea. Soon the question will be: 'What shall we eat? How shall we exist?' In Australia and America we have still plenty of room, thank God! but on the other hand our manners are not polished, and we want a great deal of the refinement for which you are conspicuous."

"I am pleased to hear you make the admission, Mr. Jarrett."

"I feel disposed to make any number of admissions, Mr. Tomlinson, only I must not take up your time by inflicting too many of my crude, colonial opinions upon you. And now, what do you say to accompanying me to the stables? A real English hunter is what I have longed all my life to behold."

The solicitor assented to this proposition, whereupon Bob and his mentor gave up arguing and proceeded direct to the stables.

CHAPTER VII.

"NOT HALF A BAD SORT OF GENT."

As is generally the case in most good hunting counties, great care and attention had been bestowed upon the equine department. The stables at Straightem Court were approached by a massive stone archway, rendered picturesque by the luxuriant ivy which clung to its walls.

This archway led into a square, neatly-tiled court-yard, round three sides of which ran the hunters' loose boxes, the remaining one being devoted to wash-houses, harness rooms, &c. The late Captain Straightem had prided himself on the number and the superior quality of his horses. No man in the whole county owned better animals or ones of a higher class.

Out of sixteen, nearly all were thorough-bred, or next door to it.

This fact, perhaps, was not remarkable in itself, but it was rendered so by every single quadruped being up to fourteen stone. And those who know anything of horseflesh will at once recognize how much time, trouble and money must have been expended by the deceased gentleman to achieve such a result.

It is far from being easily obtained.

As a rule, the class of thoroughbreds seen in the hunting field is represented by weedy screws, long and narrow, possessing handy heels and suspicious looking fore-legs. Nine times out of ten they are worthless cast-offs from the turf, who have been condemned at the very first trial, and never been allowed the chance of disgracing themselves in public.

When our friend Bob walked into the Straightem Court stables, and glanced down the long line of roomy, loose boxes, with their small-headed, satin-coated inmates, for the first time since his arrival in England he expressed himself in terms of unqualified admiration.

"Yes," he said, turning vivaciously to his companion, "you beat us here, I'll admit. Our horses are all very good in their way, but they are not a patch on these. They are a rough, ragged, common-looking lot in comparison. Not but what they can go—aye, and jump also. I'll back some of our kangaroos at home to get to the bottom of the best horse ever foaled. It's wonderful how the beggars slip over the ground. Occasionally, too, we come across timber that is real awkward. But for all this, I know quite well how very superior your English hunting is."

"I'm delighted you should think *any-thing* superior over here, Mr. Jarrett," said Tomlinson, still maintaining a tone of asperity. "You've been very hard to satisfy so far."

"Well, anyway, I'm satisfied now; I don't mind confessing how impatient I am to try my hand at some *bona-fide* fox-hunting, such as Australia cannot furnish."

"You have a stud of horses here, Mr. Jarrett, which I take it will enable you to see as much of the sport as you like. I'm no great *connoisseur* in such matters myself, but I always heard that no one was so famous for the quality of his cattle as my late respected client."

"Ah! poor chap!" exclaimed Bob, his face growing suddenly grave, "I was quite forgetting about him. Of course, never having known him makes a lot of difference; nevertheless it seems horrid of me to be looking forward to riding his gees, when he is hardly cold in his grave."

"It does strike one as rather soon, certainly," acquiesced Mr. Tomlinson.

Bob stuck his hands into his trousers pockets, and for a second appeared to be revolving some mental problem. It did not take him long to come to a solution, for in another minute he said, speaking decisively, as if to convince himself as well as his hearer :

"It's impossible to pretend to have any personal feeling for a man who is an absolute stranger to you. Of course, I am sorry my uncle's death should have occurred ; but if I were to go about in sackcloth and ashes, then I should feel like a most tremendous humbug. Besides," and his face lit up with youthful enthusiasm, " I can't help wanting to hunt when I get a chance. By-the-bye, do you happen to know when the hounds meet again ? "

" I really have no idea," returned Mr. Tomlinson disapprovingly ; for Bob's manners were not at all in accordance with his notions of what those of a gentleman occupying his client's present important position should be. "You know Matthews, no doubt?" and he turned interrogatively towards Captain Straightem's stud-groom, who up till now had stood silently by, looking at his new master with a very dubious expression of countenance.

If Matthews was anything, Matthews was conservative, and like Mr. Tomlinson, he perceived a good deal in Bob's aspect and attire not exactly in accordance with his ideas of the appearance a real " out-and-out swell " should present.

" Yes, sir," he said in answer to the lawyer's inquiry. " 'Ounds don't go out 'afore Monday week, and," *sotto-voce*, " they would not go then, if Lord Littelbrane had his way.".

" Not before Monday week ! " exclaimed Bob, with a shade of disappointment. " Then I shall be obliged to curb my impatience. However," addressing Matthews

7 *

in his quick, bright way, " I've already made up my mind which horse I shall ride."

" Indeed, sir ! " said the stud-groom, not without a touch of irony. " May I make so bold as to inquire your choice ? "

" Yes ; " said Bob, " this is the animal that takes my fancy. I don't set up for an authority, but according to my views, he's the pick of the whole basket," and so saying, he opened the door of the nearest box, in which was standing a most admirably shaped and perfectly proportioned chestnut.

" You're not far out, sir," said the old groom, with a pleased smile beginning to steal over his face. " I see as 'ow you knows a good hoss when you sees him."

" I ought to," replied Bob ; " for one way and another, I have had plenty to do with horses. What do you call this handsome fellow ? "

" Kingfisher, sir."

" And not half a bad name, though he is

such a thorough gentleman, that he ought to have been 'The King' without the 'fisher.' But, I say, " suddenly bending down and inspecting a couple of half-healed wales on the good horse's forearms, " what's the matter here? He looks as if he had been in the wars."

Matthews' naturally impassive face began to twitch.

" This, sir," he said, in a curiously subded voice, " is the animal on which Captain Straightem met his death. King-fisher was his favourite mount—and rightly so—for a finer hunter never looked through a bridle. But," with a sigh, " the hoss has got a bad name now, and I'm afraid it will stick to him all his life, though he don't deserve it—not one bit. It was no fault of his that the master came to grief; and, I tell you, sir, I went to look at the fence. I could see the hoof-marks where Kingfisher took off; but that there infernal wire was quite three yards away from the hedge. No animal living could have cleared it. But— there—there, I can't bear to think of it all."

And so saying, Matthews, totally over- come by the recent sad occurrence, and by the stigma which he imagined would attach to his favourite horse henceforth and for ever, turned sharply away so as to hide two great tears that were coursing slowly down his weatherbeaten cheeks.

Up till now Bob had taken somewhat of a dislike to the man. He fancied he was airified and stuck-up ; but as he listened to the husky tones in which Matthews con- cluded the above speech, his heart grew suddenly soft, and yielding to a kindly impulse, he laid his hand on the old groom's shoulder.

" Look here, my man," he said, glancing down at him with a pair of bright, yet compassionate eyes, " you don't cotton over and above much to me, I know. One always feels these sort of things without being told 'em. From all I hear, you have had a very good master, and therefore I, for one, say you are quite right not to welcome a new one in too much of a hurry."

" It ain't that exactly, sir," interrupted Matthews, with evident embarrassment ; " leastways, not altogether."

" Well, never mind ; we need not go into all the ins and outs just now, but I can make a pretty shrewd guess as to your feelings, and, by jingo, were I in your place I should feel exactly the same. Moreover, Matthews, I can see quite plainly that you're not easy in your mind about King-fisher. You think after what has happened, I shall probably want to sell him."

" Oh, sir, but you've just guessed my thoughts entirely," and once more Matthews' eyes began to blink suspiciously, whilst he cleared his throat with evident effort.

" Now look here," said Bob, " I daresay
I'm very far from being the sort of master
you have been accustomed to; but that
ain't my fault any more than it is yours. I
may be rough; nevertheless, when I say a
thing I mean it; and I give you my word
of honour that the chestnut shall never pass
into strange hands. I know without being
told what a good horse he is. I will keep
him and ride him fairly, just as if all this
bad business had never happened; and
when he gets too old for work, and past
picking up a comfortable livelihood in the
green fields, then we'll just send a bullet
through the poor fellow's head and put him
out of his misery. There, does that satisfy
you? " and Bob looked the stud-groom
straight in the face.

All of a sudden, Matthews seized Bob's
hand and began jerking it up and down,
exactly as if he were at work on a pump-
handle.

This process lasted several seconds. At last he found ·voice enough to say huskily :

" God bless you, sir, for those kind words. They show that you have got a good heart. And it would just about have broken me down to have seen the best horse in this, or any county, put up for sale at public auction. I bred him myself ; handled and broke him in. Nobody except me and my poor master ever knew how good he was. Oh, dear ! oh, dear ! the thought of losing Kingfisher as well as Captain Straightem has pretty nigh drove me mad," and he wiped his brow with a red cotton handkerchief.

" My poor old chap, don't give the matter another thought. I have promised not to sell the horse, and nothing shall induce me to do so."

And so saying, Bob, who was himself beginning to feel a little affected by

Matthews' emotion, left the stables and strolled leisurely towards the house.

Matthews looked after him long and critically.

"Yes," he muttered to himself, " he may be a bit rough—in fact, he *is* rough. There ain't one man in a thousand as has got the · captain's beautiful, soft, lazy manner; but for all that, he's not half a bad sort of gent. Anyway, I intend to do my dooty by him and be all on the square. I'll let no one rob him if I can help it."

And later on, if Matthews ever heard a disparaging word about Bob uttered in his presence, he always looked severely at the offender, and said :

" You're talking of what you know nothing about. Now I can tell you for a fact that Mr. Jarrett is a truer gentleman than many of those as thinks a lot more of themselves and is not half so good in reality."

CHAPTER VIII.

LONGING FOR A RIDE.

A WEEK passed slowly away, and never in his life had Robert P. Jarrett, Esq., felt more thoroughly bored and altogether miserable. His new prosperity sat uneasily upon him. He missed the simple laborious open air life to which he had been accustomed. If he attempted to do the most ordinary thing for himself, he found that there was nearly always, within arm's reach, some individual whose duty it was to perform that thing, and who felt aggrieved and astonished by " The Master" encroaching upon his or her rights and privileges.

To be thus waited upon, might soon

have grown bearable to one unaccustomed
to luxury, had the particular thing only
been well done.   But this it never was.

To take one small instance amongst
many.

Bob had always been in the habit of
sharpening his own razors.   It is possible
that they were not invariably perfectly
stropped, but at any rate, he sharpened
them to his entire satisfaction.   But now
he was no longer allowed to continue this
practice.   The gentleman of the padded
calves took charge of his shaving apparatus,
and professed to honour it with his personal
supervision.   The consequence was that
never before had Bob's chin suffered to
such an extent.   Hardly a morning passed
without its receiving some injury of a painful and unsightly nature.

His clothes were another source of
annoyance.

They were constantly being folded up

and put away in drawers and cupboards whose very existence he knew nothing of. To find any particular garment was like looking for a needle in a barrel of bran. It was enough for him to place an entirely clean pocket handkerchief in his pocket over night to discover it, after a long search, deposited next morning in the dirty linen basket, along with socks worn for three or four hours only, collars that had not a stain or a disfiguring mark upon them, and shirts that looked as if they had just returned from the washerwoman's hands.

Now these things, although trifles, were trifles utterly opposed to Bob's habits, principles and education. He had a horror of waste, but more especially of that waste so seldom considered, *i.e.*, the needless expenditure of human labour and of human vitality. His theory was, that people should use their heads and save their hands.

"*Think* what you have got to do, and
then do it!" he often said to the men
employed on his farm; "but never put
out your strength needlessly. For instance,
I drop a handkerchief and a knife out of
my pocket; if I am wise, I pick them both
up together. The one action of stooping
answers a double purpose; but a foolish
man will pick up first the one and then the
other. Instead of bending down once, he
bends twice, and by so doing expends
physical force, which with a very little
consideration might have been economized."

Bob's theories were, no doubt, all very
well in their way, but he had not been
four and twenty hours in the mother
country before discovering that, when
tested, they were practically useless. It
seemed to him that many of the lower
classes in England had never been *taught* to
think. At least, that was the only way he
could account for their stupidity. As

for the domestic servants at Straightem Court, they almost maddened him. One and all lived in a little narrow groove, filling their stomachs and starving their intellects, and performing their daily tasks without an atom of forethought or intelligence.

Perhaps it was because Bob had been brought up as a very poor man that habits of waste, luxury and expenditure did not come easily to him when he suddenly found himself placed in the position of a rich one.

To have plenty of money at one's command, no doubt was pleasant; but there were certain accompaniments of fortune which appeared almost intolerable to the simply reared Australian.

And amongst the most intolerable, strange to say, he classed his daily meals.

To eat breakfast, luncheon and dinner in stately solitude, and be solemnly stared at and execrably waited upon by a couple ot stolid men-servants, was almost more than he could stand. Over and over again he felt as if he *must* jump up from the table—they were so horribly slow—and just take what he wanted, independent of the fuss and the dignity and the needless procrastination. It set every nerve on tension, and filled him with a mad desire to kick butler and footman out of the room, and dispense with their services altogether.

At such times he felt extremely home-sick and his thoughts would wander off to the pleasant, sociable meals of Australia. In his mind's eye he could see his mother sitting at one end of the table, smiling tenderly at him. He could see himself occupying the seat opposite, and all the bright, eager, healthy, happy faces of his young brothers and sisters, as they crowded round the board and looked up to him as the head of the family.

Once more he heard the merry hum of voices and peals of light-hearted laughter, mixing with the clatter of knives and forks, whilst from the oldest to the youngest each tried to supply not only his own, but also his neighbour's wants. There was little enough of ceremony about those dinners. And yet how jolly they were! How entirely free from silly, unmeaning conventionality. Bob told himself he would rather eat a mutton chop over there than partake of Lord Mayor's fare at Straightem Court; in fact, he became so nervous, that he positively dreaded the long, dull stately banquets, eaten amidst outward surroundings of magnificence, but with an inward sense of intense discomfort and annoyance.

True, he had only to express a wish for the men-servants to retire; but that was precisely what he dared not do. He knew he was raw, he knew he was ignorant, and in his innermost heart burned a consuming

ambition in all things to imitate the habits
and customs of a real county gentleman.

" If I am to live here in future," he
mused, with the common sense characteristic
of him, " I must get to be one of them.
I can tell by my own feelings that I've
got the deuce of a lot to learn. It's queer
that so many of these English habits should
go so much against the grain with me, but
I'll force myself to fall in with them all the
same."

It was a brave resolution, rendered the
more so because he had to exercise an
immense amount of will-power to put it
into force, besides · a good deal of self-
control, and what—to him—was personal
inconvenience.

Liberty had been the one predominating
feature of his Colonial life. The bonds
imposed by civilization had hitherto sat
lightly upon him. He was a child of the
soil, of the sun, of the sky, of the wind ;

and as such, free and unconventional. To speak the truth and do your duty appeared to him better than all the most subtle and specious of religions.

And now he felt cramped and limited, like a man confined in a strait jacket. He panted for air, for space. England seemed to him great and yet small: great in her commercial activity, her factories, her vast and busy emporiums; but small, in that she could not see how her love of comfort, of luxury and pleasure, was like the Romans of old, slowly but surely bringing about her downfall. The nation wanted rousing; like an over-fed child, it was surfeited and sick.

Then in the midst of these tragically severe reflections, Bob's mind would dart off again to home. He thought of his favourite sister; dear, bright-eyed, good-natured Belle, who was always ready with sympathy on every occasion, and to whom

8*

he invariably confided all his sorrows and disappointments. Little Tottie too, with her rosy face, and comical upturned nose. How he wished they were with him. He began to long for somebody to talk to. For Mr. Tomlinson had left, and Bob, who was not accustomed to his own society, quickly wearied of it and pined for companionship.

He missed the occupations of his everyday life on the farm ; and unacquainted as yet with his new duties, he wandered aimlessly about from house to stable, from stable to garden, and from garden to outbuildings.

He would have given a ten pound note to set to work and dress a horse, dig a potato bed, or round up the cattle in the big green undulating fields.

But although Englishmen might condescend to such occupations in other countries, they could not do so in their own. Caste and custom equally forbade it.

At last this long, long week came to an end, and the meets of the Morbey Anstead hounds were once more advertised in the papers.

Bob's spirits rose as he conned them over; the depression which had crept upon him vanished. Once more he was all eagerness and expectation.

His intense wish to go out with a first-rate pack of English fox-hounds, and judge for himself what the national sport was really like, at length appeared in a fair way of being fulfilled. He looked forward to this novel experience with all the ardour of a child.

November the fifteenth broke very differently from November the first.

The one day had been made up of gloom and fog, the other was as brilliant as a blue sky and clear sunshine could render it.

A soft air blew, the fields were vividly green, the hedgerows only just beginning to change colour, and but for a few fluttering leaves falling with light irregular motion to the ground, one might have fancied that summer was still lingering, loth to take a seven months' farewell of Mother Earth.

On this eventful morning Bob woke early, and spent an unusual time over his toilet. To tell the truth, until now he had never given it a thought.

But alas! there were many difficulties in the way such as he had not dreamt of.

These, perhaps, may be better understood when it is hinted that he possessed neither breeches nor boots. The necessity of such articles had not occurred to him, and even now he did not consider them to be of very paramount importance.

But his state of mental serenity soon received a severe shock.

Charles the solemn, Charles the lethargic, Charles the padded, was he who dealt the blow. He informed his master that without such articles of costume he could not possibly be seen in the hunting field.

" Why, bless my heart alive," expostulated Bob, with considerable animation, " when we go kangaroo chasing in Australia we none of us care twopence what we wear. We think only of the sport, not of our clothes."

" Yes, sir, I suppose so, sir," answered Charles, not yielding an inch from the position he had assumed.

" Why ! have you ever been out there ? " asked Bob quickly.

" No, sir ; never, sir."

" Then what made you say, ' I suppose so.' "

" Because," said Charles with a huge accession of dignity, " I himagined that them sort of way was good enough for

the Colonies, but they don't do over here.
Gents is more pertikler."

"How do you mean? I don't quite
understand."

"They likes to *look* like gentlemen," responded Charles unsympathetically.

This answer had an exceedingly dispirit-
ing effect upon Bob. He wondered what
Charles meant by it? Did he intend to
say that no man could look like a gentleman unless he wore boots and breeches
out hunting, or was the remark applicable
only to himself?

"What the dickens am I to do, then?"
he enquired despondently.

Charles scratched his head; an operation
which apparently furnished him with an
idea.

"Couldn't you get into some of Captain
Straightem's breeches?" he suggested.
"You and he are about of a size, though
you ain't shaped exactly alike."

But Bob firmly repudiated this notion.

It seemed to him quite sufficient to step into the dead man's shoes, inherit his property, and ride his horses. He drew the line at wearing his clothes. There was something unnatural and repulsive in the thought.

"No, no; of course I couldn't," he answered indignantly. "I'd sooner cut my throat first. Don't mention it again." And he looked sternly at Charles.

The latter, though infinitely disgusted, gave up the point, but not before he had succeeded in detracting considerably from Bob's pleasure, and making him feel on thoroughly bad terms with himself.

Finally, after much hesitation, and still more perplexity, Susan the housemaid was politely called for, and requested to sew on two elastic straps to the hem of Bob's everyday trousers. With this contrivance, he devoutly hoped his pantaloons would stop in their place.

Nevertheless, a species of subdued irritation pervaded his being.

Charles' remarks had left their sting, and the supercilious smile which wreathed his fat and oily countenance, whilst the straps were being adjusted, still further served to incense Bob and to increase his anxieties as to his " get-up."

He had very little personal vanity, perhaps because as yet it had never been called into play. Clothes, as clothes, had not formed one of the chief studies of his life, as they do of the modern " Masher."

The cut of his coat, the sit of his collar, the glaze of his cuffs, and elegance of his cane, had seldom given him more than a passing thought ; but now, all at once, he began to conceive of the immense benefits which such important items confer upon a man moving, or aspiring to move, in good

English society. When, eventually, he sallied forth, he could not help confessing to himself that even Charles' opinion carried weight. He would have felt many degrees easier in his mind could he but have been convinced of that individual's approval instead of his undisguised scorn.

The influences of the mother country were already at work; and Bob was soon destined to learn how important a factor dress is in the hunting field, and how often by it, and it alone, men are judged, accepted or rejected.

Ties, bows, buttons, breeches. Who can affect to despise ye?

Across Bob's mind flashed a little incident, which long ago he remembered having read in some English magazine. The words recurred to him vividly.

"A man once came out hunting who did not see fit to wear a white collar. In its place he sported a blue spotted comforter, which he wound several times round his thick purple neck. Now that man never got on. He was cut by the county. Nobody knew him. Nobody dreamt of asking him to dinner. The reason? Oh! the reason was simple enough. The comforter damned him. He might have been ever so good a fellow, but not a soul would take the trouble to find out what a person was like who was rash enough to dispense with white collars."

This passage seemed, under present circumstances, so well adapted to himself, that Bob's spirits sank away to nothing at all.

Thank goodness! he *had* on a well glazed collar, but then it was of a turn down shape, which Charles strongly condemned; and to make matters worse, his tie was blue, and spotted also.

As for his nether limbs, when he thought of those two elastic straps, and how all his

enjoyment and moral peace depended upon
their standing the strain to which they
were subjected, he really had not courage to
glance at them.

He could not refrain from gloomy mis-
giving.

For what if they were to give way ? In
what position should he then be placed ?
Torturing visions of creased socks, shortened
trousers, and white legs, rose to his mind
and thrilled it with unutterable dismay.

But he was fairly started now, and of all
his retainers, old Matthews had been the
only one to administer a crumb of comfort.

Bob, as already related, desired to ride
Kingfisher, but Kingfisher's wounds were
not yet healed, and Matthews had recom-
mended a fine, upstanding bay in his place,
named The Swell.

" Is he a good 'un ? " asked Bob with
some curiosity.

" Yes, sir, a ripper, particularly at timber.

You can ride him with confidence. He has but one fault."

"Any objection to stating it, Matthews?"

"No, sir, not in the least. He won't face water."

"Oh! won't he. The beggar! Not even if he is made to?"

"Not even if he is made to," responded Matthews gravely. "The man who rode him last was not one to put up with any denial. 'Owever, we have so few brooks in these parts that The Swell's little peequliarity don't so much signify."

So Bob mounted his hunter and rode off.

He was accustomed to horse exercise, and had constantly been in the habit of galloping from one end of his farm to the other, but he was *not* accustomed to the easy paces and springy action of the animal he now for the first time bestrode.

In ten minutes he had forgotten all about the vexations with which his day had begun. As he entered a grass field, and let The Swell stride along over the ridge and furrow, he thought that in his whole life he had never experienced a more perfect and exhilarating sensation.

He had decided to ride his hunter out to covert, the meet being within a couple of miles of Straightem Court. But short as was the distance, it proved sufficient to put him on good terms with The Swell, and inspire him with confidence in his mount.

As he trotted down a long, straggly street, bordered on either side by small shops and unevenly built cottages, which went by the name of Morton village (the fixture for the day), and watched the women and children clustering round the doorways, a smile spread slowly over his countenance.

Everything was new to him ; everything

a source of interest, wonderment or amusement.

Unconscious of the fiat which had gone forth against him in the names of Lord Littelbrane and General Prosieboy, he looked forward with keen delight to his introduction to an English field and to a pack of well-bred, well-trained English fox-hounds.

Every nerve in his body was quivering with suppressed excitement.

It seemed to him that surely this would prove a red-letter day in his life, ever to be looked back upon with gratifying recollections.

Poor, foolish young man ! He had yet to learn that no pleasure equals the pleasure of anticipation—that joyous picturing of the imagination, which stern reality strips of its fancies, just as approaching winter strips the pretty many-coloured hedgerows.

CHAPTER IX.

WELCOMING THE STRANGER.

Of the natural stiffness of county gentlemen, their reserve towards strangers, their
curious reluctance to make fresh acquaint-
ances, their distrust of every one who is
not at least the friend of a friend, a scion
of the aristocracy, or furnished with un-
deniable credentials Bob knew absolutely
nothing. Cliques and coteries were to him
empty, meaningless words.

Where he came from, such nice distinc-
tions had not yet been introduced.

He had a kind of an idea that people
who went out hunting were all "hail
fellow, well met"; the sport united them in
bonds of sympathy and companionship;
the farmer was as good as the lord, the

tradesman as the farmer. At least, such were Bob's notions.

They showed how ignorant he was, and how extremely little he knew of the Morbey Anstead Hunt. Democratic views were sternly suppressed by that self-approving body of gentlemen known as the Mutual Adorationites.

When Bob reached the end of the village, he found the cottages widened out on either side in order to inclose a small triangular-shaped common of about two acres in extent. Here, of a summer's evening, the lads assembled in great force, pitched their wickets and enjoyed a good game of cricket.

Just now, the point of attraction proved to be a neat little whitewashed inn, over whose door hung a large and brilliantly painted signpost. Its yard was full of horses standing champing at their bits, or stamping restlessly as the groom in attendance tightened up the girths, preparatory to the mounting of his master or mistress. The hounds had already arrived and were congregated on the grass, some rolling, some playing, some placidly waving their fine-pointed sterns to and fro.

Burnett stood in their midst, mounted on a powerful, blood-like brown gelding, whilst the first whip occasionally made the lash of his hunting crop crack with a resounding noise, when an inquisitive hound, more excitable and less obedient than his comrades, ventured outside the circle.

The old ones, who knew what they had come out for, were mostly sensible enough, but now and again, a youthful member of the establishment, possessing an active canine mind, would exhibit a propensity to make acquaintance with horses' legs, or sniff suspiciously at the knots of little sturdy boys and girls who stood watching the proceedings, half in fear, half in delight.

9*

Then the thong descended on the offender's hind quarters, and sent him yelping back from whence he came, smarting under a sense of injury. Bob pulled up his horse, and watched these and similar incidents with keen interest. Nothing escaped him. He noticed the sleekness of the hounds' coats, and what an admirably matched lot they were. He looked down into the depths of their honest, wistful eyes, that appeared now yellow, now brown, now luminously red, according to how the sunlight fell upon them.

Mongrels he had seen by the score; but never such hounds as these. It was a delight to watch them; each movement betrayed high pedigree. One sedate and curiously marked fellow particularly took his fancy. He was a very light hound, almost white, save for a few patches of tan, and he lay on the grass, as if determined not to distress himself until necessary, with his noble head reposing contentedly on out-stretched paws, stained to a dark hue by the muddy roads along which he had travelled.

"Is that a good hound?" asked Bob of one of the whips.

"The best killer in the pack, sir. He comes from Lord Lonsdale."

And now people began to arrive from every quarter. The little common was dotted over with red coats, thrown up by a sprinkling of black. The sun shone out and made the brass buttons twinkle like miniature stars; it cast a sheen on the horses' smooth coats, bringing their strong muscles into high relief, and lighting up the whole stir-ring and varied scene with its clear, genial rays. Overhead was a soft blue sky, across whose broad expanse of tender azure floated a few gossamer clouds, misty and white, their snowy purity contrasting vividly with the distant ether.

Bob—who was naturally observant—thought that, taking it altogether, he had never looked upon so goodly a sight.

He no longer wondered at the pride and enthusiasm Englishmen displayed when talking of fox-hunting. He could fully sympathize with their feelings.

For even as he gazed at the bright array, a glow of exultation thrilled his veins. In fact, he was so absorbed by all he now saw for the first time, that he did not notice a small group of well mounted, well-appointed men who had drawn near and were evidently criticizing the new-comer's appearance.

Perhaps it was just as well that he escaped seeing the smiles of mingled indignation and contempt which disfigured their countenances, as they stood there and took stock of their fellow-creature.

Luckily for Bob, it did not enter his head to imagine that he was furnishing subject of amusement. To tell the truth, he had clean forgotten all about those unfortunate elastic straps. The excitement of the moment had chased their memory away.

Besides, he also was engaged in making mental observations, and had already taken a rapid survey of the assembled field.

Some few elegant sportsmen he marked down in his mind's tablet as " real swagger chaps, regular out-and-out swells." Needless to say these were the Mutual Adorationites. Others again appeared to be good fellows, without an atom of " side."

Yet, curiously enough, Bob's instinctive desire was to make acquaintance with the former rather than with the latter class. Chiefly because these extra-refined indi- viduals were rarities in his Colonial life, hitherto seldom met with ; and also because he had a notion they possessed a certain amount of originality and constituted a type altogether novel in his experiences. Perhaps, too, some inward consciousness whispered that they belonged to an entirely different order—the order to which, by his uncle's death, he ought now to aspire. No doubt they could teach him manners. For manners, above all, were what humble-minded Bob told himself he was sadly deficient in. His heart might be good, his sentiments irreproachable, but what was the use of that without fine old British polish? He was determined to lose no opportunity of acquiring it.

Meantime, Lord Littelbrane gave the signal for a move to be made, and hounds were at once trotted off at a brisk pace to draw Neverblank Covert, whose name was suggestive of the good sport it invariably afforded.

It lay on the slope of a hill, removed

from roads and railways, and was situated in a scantily populated portion of the county. The strong, healthy gorse of which it was composed afforded a retreat dear to the vulpine race ; and dire was the disappointment if by any chance Neverblank failed to furnish a fox when called upon. As a rule, the chief difficulty consisted in dislodging the quarry ; for owing to the stoutness of the gorse, it was by no means an easy covert for hounds to draw.

But to-day they were fresh and eager, and in their ardour heeded not the stabs inflicted on their fine skins by the sharp-pointed prickles. By the end of five minutes no less than three foxes were viewed stealing across the rides.

" Hoick, my beauties. Hoick, hoick at 'em," called out Burnett encouragingly, in a mellow, resonant voice that could be heard from afar.

Nevertheless, a considerable delay occurred, during which our friend Bob was on the tip-toe of expectation.

Once three or four young hounds appeared for a few minutes, and gave chase to a startled hare. Bob immediately joined in the pursuit, but to his intense disappointment, up rode the first whip and administered to the offenders such a punishment that they were only too glad to effect a retreat, their sense of guilt weighing heavily upon them.

As for Bob, not being a hound, he was castigated by the human tongue instead of by the lash. To his consternation, he suddenly found himself addressed by a stout, white-haired, red faced, choleric-looking old gentleman, who at that moment bore a curious resemblance to an infuriated turkey-cock, thanks to the wobbling muscles of his purple throat.

"God d——n it, sir! Where the devil

are you going to?" he roared out at the top of his voice, glaring fiercely at Bob with his small glittering eyes.

"I thought we were going to have a run," answered the young man apologetically.

"The deuce you did, and pray," blankety blankety, blank—the reader's ear must not be offended by too faithful a repetition of the general's language—" what the dickens do you mean by encouraging Lord Littelbrane's hounds to run riot? Eh! answer me that question." And once more his flabby, pendulous throat became convulsed.

"I didn't intend to do anything wrong or against the rules," said Bob meekly. "But I fancied we were off."

"Off! indeed. You seem to possess a lively fancy, sir ; rather too lively when combined with so *very*," he laid a sneering emphasis on the word, "small knowledge of hunting. But you've made a mistake, let me tell you. The Morbey Anstead don't go in for teaching beginners how to hunt. You had far better try some other pack, for *we*,"—oh! the importance, the majesty and superiority contained in that word — " expect people to behave themselves when they come out with us."

This speech angered Bob not a little; still with an effort he stifled his wrath. He had no wish to enter into a quarrel, but more especially did he dislike squabbling with a man so many years his senior. He determined to try the effect of a soft answer.

" I beg pardon," he said quietly but firmly. " I had no idea that I had committed so gross a breach of etiquette as, according to you, I unfortunately appear to have done."

But General Prosieboy was not one to be easily appeased. After the conversation which had taken place between himself and

Lord Littelbrane he felt as if his personal honour were at stake, and that he was bound, not only as a gentleman, but also as a M.A., to crush Bob down to the very ground. If his opponent had flown into a temper he would have been more at ease. The young man's humble, yet at the same time manly, manner was just a trifle disconcerting. He must not let his rage evaporate.

" Damnation, sir," he retorted irately. " *You* had no idea, indeed ! Pray what excuse is that? None, none whatever. It cannot be permitted that you should ruin our hounds and spoil our day's sport. People have no right to come out hunting with a pack like the Morbey Anstead when they don't even know the difference between a fox and a hare."

Bob reddened. The speaker's manner was so intentionally offensive that he realized at last that this foul-tongued old gentleman was deliberately setting to work to insult him. He was a high-spirited young fellow, and having once arrived at this conclusion, no longer made any effort to conceal his indignation.

"Will you be good enough to tell me who you are and what your name is?" he inquired with considerable heat.

Blankety—blank. "What's that to you?" replied the general.

"A great deal. I wish to know if you are authorized to keep the Field in order, and for what purpose you disgrace yourself by using bad language."

"Damn it, sir. Do you mean to tell me that you question my authority and wish to know my name?"

"You have guessed my desire correctly."

"By gad! sir, I'm not ashamed of it," returned the other excitedly. "It's Prosieboy, General Prosieboy."

"A very applicable name, no doubt,"

said Bob, with a sarcasm he could not refrain from.

" And as for my authority," continued the general, treating this remark with the contempt it deserved, and inflating himself like a balloon filled full of pride instead of gas, "you need be under no apprehension about *that*. I am Lord Littelbrane's most intimate friend, and every action of mine invariably meets with his concurrence."

On such an occasion, when he was fighting the battles of the whole sacred body of Mutual Adorationites, General Prosieboy's conscience told him that it was a gallant and virtuous thing to draw the long bow. The young man had to be suppressed and squashed. At present he showed no signs of submission.

"I presume then," said Bob, with a twinkle in his eye, for General Prosieboy's grandiose manner had an irresistibly comic effect upon him, " that his lordship is by

no means particular with whom he asso-
ciates and has not an easily offended ear."

And so saying Bob galloped off at full
speed, for a loud "gane forrard awa-ay"
rang through the air, repeating itself in
many sounding echoes. This time the fox
really took to his heels, and he, Bob, had
not a moment to lose.

General Prosieboy stood for a second
and looked after him. Then he shook his
head doubtingly.

"He ought to be settled—he ought to be
settled," he· muttered three or four times
over in tones full of anxiety and dissatis-
faction. "And yet ——" with an oath,
"I'm not sure that he is. Mr. Robert P.
Jarrett is just about as tough a customer
as I've come across for a long time. However, if he feels inclined to show fight I'll
have another shy at him by-and-bye."
Whereupon he clapped spurs to his horse
and rode off for the nearest road.

CHAPTER X.

CUTTING THEM ALL DOWN.

"WELL I'm blowed," said Bob to himself, as The Swell glided over the pastures with his long, smooth stride. "That old cove's boots and breeches were perfection, and yet I wonder if he is a specimen of the sporting gentleman. If so, they must be an uncommonly queer lot."

But General Prosieboy soon vanished from his thoughts, for the hounds were straight ahead, running hard and mute, whilst the Field were already split up into half-a-dozen different divisions. The Swell, too, was pulling like one not accustomed to the indignity of seeing many of his own species in advance of him. Bob let him go, being also anxious to get to the front as quickly as possible.

Although, thanks to his recent encounter, he had not been particularly fortunate in securing a start, he soon made the pleasing discovery that, owing to the extraordinary speed of his horse, he was only cantering when others were galloping, and before very long he succeeded in joining the leading horsemen.

This position contented him, and he resolved if possible to maintain it. As before stated, he was accustomed to riding, and what he wanted in judgment he made up in " pluck " and dash. Although The Swell missed the delicate handling—the artistic lengthening and shortening of the reins to which he had grown accustomed when carrying his late master—he quickly ascertained that his present one was not to be denied. The good hunter's desire was to be where he could see the hounds. Bob's

wishes were identical, and as he had the
sense to leave The Swell pretty well alone
at his fences, they got on better than might
have been expected.

They had already flown some six or
seven obstacles and had established a
friendly communication. Bob's spirits rose
almost to the ecstatic pitch. His heart
beat fast. Through his veins ran a warm
glow that pervaded his whole frame and
rendered him, for the time being, insen-
sible to danger. Up to this point the
fencing had been comparatively easy. But
now they came to a narrow gap, blocked
entirely by a huge fallen tree.

The leaders pulled up and looked at it
dubiously. Somebody even suggested
dismounting and trying to force the
stubborn branches aside. Bob laughed in
his sleeve. This was the species of jump
with which he was most familiarized. That
bare, brown trunk, with its spreading

10*

stems shooting between four and five feet in the air, had no terrors for him.

He gave The Swell a touch of the spurs. No, to be correct, it was more than a touch. He intended the application to be of the gentlest possible nature, but somehow the rowels remained fixed in the animal's sides and the next moment they were over, though not without a scramble.

Still, he had shown these hard-riding Morbey Anstead gentlemen that the thing was possible to jump, and before many seconds had gone by he was joined by Burnett. At length, after the branches had been considerably beaten down, several other Nimrods hardened their hearts, whilst the timid went off in search of a gate.

Lord Littelbrane was one of those who had viewed Bob's performance.

" He's a deuce of a fellow to ride, that nephew of Straightem's," he observed to General Prosieboy, as the road division joined them. "A deuce of a fellow, though he knows nothing whatever about it."

"I'll tell you what he can do as well," said the general with venomous animation.

"What's that?" inquired his lordship apprehensively.

"Talk. He'd talk a dog's hind leg off. Take my advice, my lord, and don't give him the chance of getting in a word."

"I don't mean to."

"That's right. I had a tussle with him this morning, and he's simply impossible. Much more so even than I thought."

"Did you give it to him, Squasher?"

"I did," responded the general grimly. "But he's not had enough yet. He is one of those gentlemen who require a second dose."

"One is enough as a rule, is it not?" said his lordship, with a faint smile.

" It is, but I shall take care to make number two a very great many degrees stronger."

Meanwhile, Bob was superlatively happy. Every yard that the fox continued running he became increasingly alive to the merits of the animal he bestrode. No wonder, then, he was pleased, for it takes such a combination of qualities to make a good hunter. A single one goes for so little. The fencing is of no use without the speed, or the speed without the staying, and even then, bad manners will often destroy the whole. In short, a horse who possesses every desideratum is almost as hard to find as a pretty woman destitute of vanity, or an ugly one who is not soured.

Fence after fence The Swell threw behind him without a mistake. There are few sensations more delightful than bearing down on a good big place, finding your horse come at it exactly in his stride, and feeling by intuition before he takes off that you are safe to get over well.

The Swell was fresh and in an extra good humour. So far, nothing had occurred to put him out. The ditches were dry and no gleam of obnoxious water offended his eye. Bob's confidence increased momentarily.

Thirty glorious minutes—minutes full of concentrated enjoyment—had elapsed since the fox broke covert. But the pace had burst him, and he now held out signals of distress. Burnett's sharp eyes spied him stealing wearily down a hedge-row, carrying his brush low and his head outstretched, yet with every faculty intent on making his escape.

But how to get into the same field?

The fence that surrounded it was absolutely unjumpable. It consisted of a huge bullfinch, black as Erebus, some eight or ten feet in height and bordered on either side by a stiff ox rail.

The boldest Nimrod present recognized that it would be sheer lunacy to attempt such a leap. There was but one means of ingress, namely, through a five-barred gate, but this proved to be securely chained and padlocked. With the smallest possible delay a couple of horsemen dismounted and endeavoured to take the gate off its hinges. No, it would not yield an inch. The assembled group were done. They stood looking at the timber barrier in dismay, whilst hounds burst into a bloodthirsty chorus and raced across the green sward. Burnett cursed the fate that had mounted him on a horse bad at rails. He hesitated and his companions hesitated too. Even in the far-famed Shires, a five-barred gate is a thing not often jumped, but it is done sometimes, and generally either by a well-known bruiser or else by a complete novice   There was one novice present who felt desperate, and who moreover was in a state of such intense physical ecstasy as rendered him impervious to fear.

" Make way," he called out excitedly. And then he rode resolutely at the gate.

For a brief second, The Swell did not seem altogether certain whether his rider were in earnest. The next, reassured by that subtle electric current which surely exists between man and horse and speechlessly communicates to each, the other's intention, he cocked his small ears and gathered himself well together.

Then with a powerful twist of his hind quarters, he flung over the gate, just tapping it lightly with one hoof, and landed safely on the other side. It was both high and stiff, and Bob, conscious of the difficulty of the jump, cast a hasty backward glance to see who intended following in his wake.

But nobody showed any disposition to

emulate his example, especially as the leading hounds were already beginning to
turn.

Lord Littelbrane watched Bob's performance in silence. If there was one
thing he respected more than another it
was courage; perhaps because he suspected a deficiency of that quality in his
own nature, although nothing would have
induced him to admit the fact. Something
very like a tear gathered in his dull blue
eyes.

He turned away, and as he did so, almost
came into collision with General Prosieboy.

"Prosieboy," he said mournfully, "I
have never felt the loss of poor, dear Harry
so much as at this moment. We have
nobody left to ride for us now."

"Why, my lord! What's the matter?"

"The matter!" he replied in tones of
indescribable misery. "That terrible
person"—a shudder went through his

delicate frame—" that nephew of Harry's, has just jumped a five-barred gate and cut us all down."

"The devil he has! Well, I'm not surprised to hear it. He's mad enough for anything."

"Yes, but not another man dared follow. Even Burnett turned away."

"And quite right, too," said General Prosieboy, who was by no means an advocate of risking one's neck through the taking of hazardous leaps.

" It's a shameful thing to let this Colonial fellow take the shine out of all our best men," returned Lord Littelbrane. Then, with an unwonted burst of emotion, he added : "Oh ! Harry, Harry, dear old man; this would never have happened had you still been in the land of the living. The glory of the Morbey Anstead has departed."

After clearing the five-barred gate as related, Bob experienced a few moments of triumphant elation ; he leant forward and patted The Swell's bright, slender bay neck. But before many minutes his elation changed to dismay.

First, he was a little disconcerted at finding himself entirely alone. Second, he was not altogether certain how to proceed, and third, he perceived that the hounds had turned sharp back. The last circumstance was the most annoying of the three. For, as there was but one way into the field, so was there but one way out, and that the same.

Now it is one thing to charge a dangerous obstacle when the fury of the chase is upon you, when your blood is heated to almost fever pitch, and dozens of critical eyes are watching your performance, but it is a very different affair having to retrace your footsteps in solitude, perhaps doubting the wisdom of your action in the first instance. It is astonishing under such circumstances how much bigger the original leap looks.

As so often happens out hunting, it proved a case of the timid finding themselves better off than the brave. The former were now in the same field with the hounds.

Bob alone was separated from them. He glanced at the gate. There was no other possible mode of joining his companions. It looked horribly big, and to make matters worse, the take-off was now slightly up-hill, and indented by hoofmarks of cattle. He saw that he must not give himself time to think. If the thing were to be done at all, it must be done at once.

But perhaps what decided him was the sight of the noble master and his choleric old friend staring at him from their point of vantage with evident amusement.

He resolved to fall rather than let himself be laughed at by them, and sure enough, fall he did. The Swell made a gallant effort, but he tripped over some uneven ground just as he took off, and hitting the gate hard with both fore-legs, turned a complete somersault. Bob was a little shaken, but not really hurt, and soon recovered from the shock. He did not mind the disaster one bit; but what *did* get his monkey up, was seeing those two stuck-up, stand-off men close by never offer to give him the least assistance. He thought it downright ungentlemanly of them, and felt their conduct very keenly; especially as he overheard General Prosie-boy say scoffingly:

"Ha, ha! Tried to show off once too often. Glad he found out his mistake."

The other nodded his colourless head, and then they rode away together.

But if the Mutual Adorationites were not kind, others were.

A jolly, good-natured farmer immediately rushed to the rescue, saying admiringly :

"Gad, sir! But that was a gallant jump of yours, and a real nasty one into the bargain ; I hope you are none the worse for the roll?"

"Not in the least, thank you," said Bob, beginning to recover from the annoyance occasioned by Lord Littelbrane's and General Prosieboy's conduct. "And fortunately the horse is not injured either. At least, as far as I can judge."

"Ah! That's lucky, for he's a good 'un. Many's the time I have seen the late Captain Straightem ride him to hounds."

"By-the-by," said Bob, "perhaps you can tell me who that small, fair-haired, drab faced man is, speaking to General Prosieboy."

The farmer looked in the direction indicated.

"That!" he said, as if astonished at his

companion's ignorance. " Oh! that is Lord Littelbrane."

" I thought so, responded Bob. " What sort of a fellow is he ? "

" That's rayther a difficult question for me to answer, sir, seeing as how I am one of his lordship's principal tenants."

But Bob had already discovered what he wanted to know from the man's manner.

" Never mind," he said ; " I understand. If a question is difficult to answer, nine times out of ten it answers itself."

" You're uncommon sharp, sir," said his companion.

" Think so ? " said Bob. " Not sharp enough, I am afraid, to pick up good manners from your English gentleman."

With which enigmatical remark, being now fairly mounted, he rode off to rejoin the hounds, who were already a couple of fields distant.

CHAPTER XI.

GENERAL PROSIEBOY COMES TO THE FRONT.

Bob urged The Swell to his speed and soon overtook the pack. He reached them in the nick of time, for this good, bold fox, finding himself sorely pressed, after dodging round some farm premises to regain his lost wind, once more faced the open, in hopes of gaining Amberside Hill, some two or three miles further on.

The gallant fellow put on a desperate spurt. He knew it was the last of which he was capable. The country was strong and thickly fenced. For another ten minutes the fun continued fast and furious.

As if anxious to wipe out the indignity of a fall, The Swell jumped brilliantly, and completely re-established the high opinion he had hitherto held in the estimation of his rider. Such glorious excitement soon made Bob forget his resentment against Lord Littelbrane and General Prosieboy. He felt on good terms with all mankind, himself and his horse in particular.

For the hounds were in full cry now, pursuing the failing quarry with wide-open jaws, red hanging tongues, gleaming eyes, and upright bristles. Only one more field separated poor Pug from Amberside Hill. His foes were bent on pulling him down before he reached it. He was equally determined to baffle them. It meant life to him—only a mouthful of unsavoury food to them.

But though he toiled on gamely, he was now in full view, and the baying of the hounds and the yelling of his human enemies served still further to terrify and dishearten him. He just managed to creep through the last fence dividing the road from Amberside Hill, and lay down panting in the ditch, where, hidden by dead brown leaves and yellow edish, his body was almost undiscernible. If by this ruse he could but gain a few moments, then he might steal into the covert and seek the shelter of a friendly earth. His calculations proved correct, for one by one the eager hounds flashed over him and disappeared in the wood beyond.

Excited by the prospect of a near finish to so good a run, every horseman was on his mettle. They did not heed the stiff top-binder that ran through the fence, but charged it in a dozen different places.

Crash! crash! and two sportsmen bit the dust simultaneously, rolling into the road more forcibly than pleasantly.

Bob got over all right, and hearing the noise of falling bodies, turned to see who the unfortunates were. To his surprise, he perceived that the one nearest to him was no less a personage than General Prosieboy,

11*

who inspired by the universal enthusiasm, had for once ventured on so formidable a leap.

He was a stout man and a heavy, and he did not fall easily. Few people do when they weigh over fifteen stone and have passed sixty years of age. For several seconds he lay immovable. Perhaps he was more frightened than hurt, but anyhow the sight of his white hairs mingling with the dust filled Bob with a sentiment of compassion.

"Good for evil," he said to himself; and in another minute he was off his horse and lifting the general from the ground. He wiped him clean, caught his hunter, and finally—when he had ascertained that no great damage had been inflicted—helped him to remount.

All this time General Prosieboy spoke not a word. He accepted the attentions bestowed as if they were his due. At last he gathered up his reins and prepared to move on. At that moment, Bob, seized by a sudden desire for reconciliation, and also prompted by his good-natured Australian hospitality, looked up at the great M.A. with a pair of honest, pleading brown eyes, and said :

" Hullo ! old chap. Don't you think you and I might just as well be friends ? "

To do the general justice, taken by surprise, for one single moment he relented.

Perhaps Bob saw the softened expression of his face, for he continued, in tones of greater confidence : " I'm all alone, and deuced dull I find it. We have not been formally introduced to each other, but what do you say to coming and taking ' pot luck ' with me this evening at Straightem Court ? Eh ? " And as he spoke, he settled one of the general's gouty old feet in the stirrup.

But that gentleman, ashamed of his momentary weakness, and indignant with himself for having experienced it, recovered

from any temporary feeling of softness.
He now considered it incumbent upon him
to be doubly severe and repulsive in order
to atone for the lapse of dignity, which
owing to peculiar conditions, had unfortunately already taken place. He must not
let the enemy see that there was any joint
in his armour.

Consequently he drew himself up in his
saddle, protruded his chest, and fixing his
cold, gimlet-like eye on the audacious
Bob, said in a solemnly frigid voice, as
if his feelings were outraged beyond description :

"Young man, I make a point of *never*
dining with persons whose acquaintance I
have not had the pleasure of making in a
proper and orthodox manner. The fact is,
there are so many outsiders come to hunt
with these hounds that it is impossible to
be too particular. Under these circumstances I must decline the honour of taking

'pot luck' with one who is a complete stranger to me and likely to remain so."

So saying, and without uttering a single word of thanks for kindness received, he trotted off to a field close by, into which poor Reynard's body had been dragged, and was there undergoing the final obsequies. Despite every shift, his murderers had found him out.

Bob could only gaze after the general in speechless amazement.

" Darned old fool!" he exclaimed at last, with a burst of irrepressible wrath.

And yet there was something comic about the ancient warrior's behaviour too. It was so *very* VERY small, and displayed so lamentably narrow a mind. Angry as he felt at his insolence, Bob could hardly suppress a smile.

But how about these celebrated English manners, whose delicacy, refinement, and true politeness he had so often heard quoted at head-quarters? Were these them ?

Why, out in the bush, if one man behaved to another man in so gross and insolent a fashion, no name would be considered bad enough for him. But then, on the other hand, the offer of a good dinner did not come as often over there as it did here. Perhaps that fact made all the difference.

But reason it out as he might, Bob had received a tremendous shock. All his preconceived notions had been subjected to severe disillusion, an operation which whenever it takes place always leaves a feeling of soreness and blankness behind.

He had been so humble and diffident, so ready to learn of all the Englishmen he came across, simply because they possessed the inestimable advantage of being Englishmen ; and now he thought that he himself had more polish than they. He might be rough, blunt, outspoken, but he would have been ashamed to treat a fellow-creature as Lord Littelbrane and General Prosieboy had treated him.

It took him much longer this time to recover from his disappointment and indignation, and during the process he did not attempt to speak to a soul; in fact, after his experiences of the morning, he laid it down as a rule, so long as he remained in England, not to address a single person until overtures had first been made to him. He would be on the safe side, at any rate, and not expose himself to any more insults and rebuffs. But circumstances defeated this intention, and prevented him from putting it into execution.

Whilst jogging on to get to the next covert, the whole Field had to pass through a series of nasty little, awkward bridle-gates, that flew to, almost as soon as they were opened. Bob, being mortal and a man, had before now noticed a very pretty, smart-looking, little woman, attired in a scarlet jacket, a white waistcoat, and a glossy hat, from beneath which her small coquettish face peeped out very alluringly. An incident now took place that shocked all his sense of chivalry. No less than three gentlemen in succession pushed by, and allowed one of these gates to slam upon this lady, thereby preventing her from getting through and hurting her hand as she stretched it out in self-defence.

The very sight made Bob indignant. There was something so currish and unmanly about the proceeding to his mind, especially when there was not even the excuse of hounds running hard. He darted forward, held the gate open, and although several other men availed themselves of his courtesy, insisted on the lady passing through before he relaxed his hold.

So natural did this action appear to him,

that he was quite astonished to find her waiting for him on the other side.

" Thank you so much," she said in a clear, cheery voice. " It was awfully good of you letting me take your turn."

" Please don't mention such a trifle," he said in reply. " Anybody would have done it."

She shrugged her shoulders, and shot an inquiring glance in his direction.

" Are you well acquainted with the Morbey Anstead ? "

" No, this is the first time I have been out with them."

Lady De Fochsey—for it was she—smiled, and leaning confidentially towards Bob, said :

" You are Mr. Jarrett, are you not, Captain Straightem's nephew ? "

" Yes, how did you know ? "

" Never mind, perhaps I guessed. Tell me, are the ladies in your part of the world better treated than they are here ? "

"From what I have seen in your case, I should say, most certainly," said Bob emphatically.

"Ah! don't waste your indignation. The Morbey Anstead females do not expect to be made a fuss with; if they are tolerated it is all they can hope for. You see the men think such a tremendous lot of themselves, that it is impossible for them to think much of anybody else."

"So it appears," said Bob grimly. "You have hit it off exactly."

"Do you know," and she cast a side-long glance at him, "the highest compliment I have ever received from an M.A. was to be told, I was not in the way. Don't you think a woman ought to feel immensely flattered by such a speech? However well she may ride, however pretty she may be to look at, and nice to talk to, her highest reward is 'not in the way.'" And her ladyship burst into a little sarcastic laugh.

"Do you mean to tell me that such a saying is meant for praise?" asked Bob.

"Yes," she answered demurely, "from a Mutual Adorationite : very high praise."

"I don't quite understand the phrase; what does 'Mutual Adorationite' mean?"

"I won't explain, because it would take too long, and you so soon will find out for yourself. But to return to our sex. When gates out hunting are small, gentlemen in a hurry, ladies numerous, the latter go to the wall. They always do, all through life, for the simple reason that of all animals, man is the most animal, and the most selfish, woman the weakest, and the least protected."

"I am sorry you should think so badly of us," said Bob.

"I do not think badly of *you*," she replied, letting her limpid blue eyes rest full upon him. "You exerted your strength in my behalf."

To her surprise he made no immediate answer. To tell the truth, he was a little taken aback. Being flattered by a pretty woman was a novel experience.

"What are you thinking about?" she inquired a trifle pettishly. "You seem as if you had not heard what I said."

"You must excuse my apparent inattention, Miss——" and Bob stopped short, for he had not an idea whether his companion, were wife, widow, or maid.

She laughed outright.

"No, I am not a Miss, though you evidently seem to think that I ought to be one. My name is Lady de Fochsey." Then she looked at Bob, and told herself he was very well-favoured, and added softly, "widow of the late Sir Jonathan."

There could be no harm in letting him know that she was free to wed again, if so disposed.

Besides, she liked young men. Old

ones were so dreadfully prosy, and always *would* talk of themselves. There was a manly strength about Bob, combined with an honesty and good-humour of countenance, which she altogether approved of, even although his clothes were not exactly what they might be. But being a woman and he a man, she was inclined to regard this defect leniently, whereas if Bob had belonged to the same sex as herself, every article of costume would have been severely criticized. But ladies are nearly always kinder to gentlemen than to other ladies, and *vice-versâ*.

"The fact is," said Bob explanatorily, " whilst you were speaking, I was guilty of the rudeness of making comparisons between your country and mine."

"May I ask with what result?"

"Certainly. I came to the conclusion that our men would go simply wild over a pretty woman," Lady De Fochsey smiled encouragingly, and Bob, surprised at his own hardihood, added, " like yourself, for instance. Whilst over here, from all accounts, she is not half appreciated at her true value."

" Oh, yes !" she said, with a twinkle in her eye. " We are appreciated after a certain brutal fashion, but not in the chivalrous, Homeric way, of which you seem a regular champion."

" Chivalrous ! Homeric !" echoed Bob, a trifle puzzled. " I'm afraid I'm rather dull of comprehension."

" Very. Let me put my meaning clearer. Well, then, in Merry England, the pattern of philanthrophy and civilization, we are regarded in one of two lights. Either we are pretty creatures, fatted and kept sleek at our lord's pleasure, or else we are beasts of burden, who have to do all the hard work, and get none of the credit ; who screw and save at home, whilst

monsieur mon mari cuts a figure in the
world, and spends all the money on
amusing himself. "Oh, yes! I know."
And she pouted her full lips in a
provocative manner.

"No one could associate *you* with the
beast of burden," said Bob, growing bolder
as her ladyship became more gracious.

She laughed airily and changed the
conversation.

"Come," she said, giving her horse a
touch of her heel, "those tiresome hounds
are nearly out of sight. We must be
moving on."

Whereupon they put their respective
steeds into a canter, but Lady De Fochsey's
chestnut was completely outpaced by The
Swell, and further conversation was therefore carried on under difficulties. Just
then her ladyship spied Lord Littelbrane a
little way ahead.

"Good-bye, for the present," she called

out, "come and see me soon. Any one
will tell you where I live. Your aboriginal
ideas are as interesting to me as, it is to be
hoped, my English ones are to you." And
she waved the tip of her fingers.

Whereupon Bob rode on, considering he
had had his dismissal, and consoling himself
by thinking it really did not so much matter
what the men were like, when the ladies
were so very, very charming, and so entirely
free from all stiffness and ceremony.

As for calling, of course he should call,
and only too thankful for the chance.

She was undeniably pretty, although
after the first flutter of excitement had
passed, he told himself that, in spite of her
ladyship's charms, she was not altogether
" his style."

She wanted something. He was not quite
sure what ; but he fancied it was *soul*.

It was very pleasant, having agreeable
things said to one, but then the pleasant-

ness was in some degree diminished if you were not quite certain of the speaker's sincerity, and could imagine her making the same pretty little speeches to every man of her acquaintance. After the reception he had met with, it was extremely ungrateful of Bob to harbour such ideas, yet they occurred to his mind almost involuntarily.

Some inward voice seemed to warn him, that however much he might be captivated by Lady De Fochsey, he should never find in her the ideal woman, with whom some day he hoped to pass his life in perfect sympathy and community of spirit.

All the same, he was flattered by the notice she had taken of him. Besides, she was the first person, excepting Farmer Jackson, who had spoken to him in a frank and friendly fashion. She had lifted the sense of isolation that had gradually stolen over his spirit, and he felt more able now to put up with sneers and insults.

12*

CHAPTER XII.

A CHARMING WOMAN.

Lady De Fochsey had many admirers. Amongst their number it was not often she encountered one who had the keen insight to look beyond a pretty, superficial surface and seek to gauge the depths or shallows of her real character.

Hers was not an uncommon type of womanhood. A type that fluctuates between the good and the bad, and is continually being attracted and repulsed first by one, then the other. Stability is difficult to arrive at under such circumstances, and scarcely to be looked for. Without *will-power*, that much talked of thing, the human soul is but a poor vapid affair.

Lady de Fochsey was frivolous, and yet
not conscious of her frivolity; artificial to
a degree, but not purposely or intentionally
so. Her nature was light, facile, variable,
and, unfortunately for herself, it possessed
certain dramatic instincts, which all through
life made her seek for and delight in
" situations." As an actress she might
have made a reputation, since as a woman
she never could refrain from acting. She
meant no harm by it. It was only imagining the world a stage and she the player.
Occasionally some of her parts fitted in
very well. They *did* produce an effect.
At other times thay failed, and then of
course the player was abused and called a
" humbug," if not worse.

And yet, in the real sense of the word,
Lady de Fochsey was not a humbug.
She was true to the instincts implanted
within her. That they were changeable,
capricious, ever striving after sensation,

was perhaps more her misfortune than her fault. It is not given to all women to be strong and simple, to see the follies of their sex, and as much as possible stand aloof from them. There must be butterflies, even if their pretty wings are frail and liable to be smirched and stained.

Lady de Fochsey's conversation was bright and by the majority all the more appreciated from the fact of its containing no depth whatever. With her pretty face and neat figure, few ever noticed if she floundered a bit whenever the more serious topics of the day were mentioned, or got hopelessly muddled if by any chance the sciences and ologies were touched upon.

What did it matter ? Women were made to be amusing, not clever. Nobody wanted them to be cleverer than the men —it was only upsetting the long-established order of things, which worked so satis-

factorily for the male portion of crea-
tion. It is so easy to starve another person's intellect and then say, " You are a
fool," and so hard for the person thus
treated to disprove the assertion. Many
women now-a-days want a chance given
them—a chance of enlarging their education and proving the real grit of which
they are made. Lady De Fochsey had no
such ambition. She would rather lead up to
an emotional situation with a man, very
human, very weak, and if a little erring so
much the better, than aspire to the highest
knowledge. She liked experimentalizing
and finding out what chords and combina-
tions could be wrung from the masculine
nature.

About the female one she troubled herself very little, except in her own individual
case.

She considered that her duty in the world
was to smile graciously, make full use of

her china-blue eyes, pay little insincere compliments and by so doing get herself talked about as "a charming woman."

This duty she fulfilled admirably, though it must be admitted she possessed more allies amongst the men than amongst the ladies.

Taken as a general rule, the hunting-field is not a sphere calculated to develop the exchange of many intellectual ideas. When pursuing the fox, her ladyship was in her element.

To have a train of young men, no matter how vapid they might be, always dangling about her habit-skirt, rendered her supremely happy. The more the happier. It was a delight to count them up; a real grief to find that one had escaped from his allegiance. She called them her " tame cats," and was perpetually getting up pretty little scenes with them, that would have been an ornament to any private theatricals.

Act the first was invariably : " Charming
woman — love at first sight." Act the
second — " Quarrel. Charming woman
misunderstood." Act the third—" Grand
reconciliation. Charming woman more
charming than ever." Sometimes, however,
but never when she could help it, there
was a fourth act—" Break away of cap-
tive, charming woman in despair—confounded at hearing herself abused."

It is astonishing how many varieties
this little play was capable of. The chief
actor never seemed to tire, but derived
fresh amusement from every rehearsal.

All were fish that came to Lady De Fochsey's net. She welcomed Bob as a new
admirer, partly because she was already
prepossessed in his favour by the episode
of the gate, and partly owing to her own
peculiar ideas of true love.

She was always in search of true love,
yet curiously enough had never found it.

When she married the late Sir Jonathan, fat, red and wealthy, twenty years older than herself, she was persuaded the *grande passion* had come at last. It hadn't.

Two years of matrimony completely did away with the illusion as far as the baronet was concerned. Query:—Would she have entertained it if he had not had twelve thousand a year?

When Sir Jonathan died, Lady De Fochsey did not weep her eyes out. After a decent interval—it was scarcely more—she recovered from her grief.

And now! behold the beautiful confidence of the female nature. She was so romantic, so trustful and enthusiastic, that she firmly believed there was no reason, because one man had failed to answer her expectations, why another should do the same.

She had now been a widow for five years, was twenty-eight years of age, and began to feel a trifle disappointed with herself, for not having succeeded in falling in love.

She was puzzled why the *grande passion* did not arrive. She had done her best to foster it, by reading all sorts of novels of the ardent, consuming, soul-too-big-for the-body type. If anything could have kindled the required spark such literature ought to have proved successful.

It helped a little, but only a little, for the provoking part of it was, that noble and high-flown as were the theories propounded, they did not work well when applied to practical life. There was always a hitch somewhere.

The Byronic young man with dark passionate eyes, hollow cheeks and wondrous magnetic power over all the women with whom he came in contact—the young man who cared nothing for material comforts, who disdained luxury, and did not even care for a good dinner, was not to be found now-a-days. The type was dying out, and every year became more scarce. Lady De Fochsey entertained a species of veneration for it; but even she could not help admitting, in her own secret consciousness, that living on romance and sentiment, and whimsical, high-flown words, might be an exceedingly fine thing, yet when put to the actual proof, it was a still finer thing after a hard day's hunting, when you came home tired and wet, to find a nice warm room, a glowing fire and a *recherché* little repast awaiting you.

When she stretched herself out full-length on a sofa, attired in a captivating tea gown, and read one of the fashionable Spiritualistic novels on the mysteries of the occult world, astral planes, electric forces and so on, she never could quite determine in her own mind how much or how little of an impostor she was.

For she *did* like her comforts—especially when she could enjoy them in private. It was impossible to deny the fact, and what was worse, each year she seemed to like them better. But then on the other hand how exquisitely divine it must be for your amorous soul to have the power of making little celestial expeditions quite independent of its mundane body, and go flitting and flying about in search of the much-wished-for and sure-to-exist-somewhere kindred spirit.

There was something ecstatic, captivating and ennobling in the very idea.

And then the delight of the kindred spirit! The meeting, the joy, the embracing! It is to be feared that Lady De Fochsey's little head was often in a muddle. She accepted every new theory of the day, without understanding a single one.

The conflict going on between her body and her soul verged on the pathetic.

She could not make up her mind whether to throw in her lot with things heavenly or things earthly. They both had their fascinations, and the struggle was terrible.

When she found disappointment in the one, she had recourse to the other. But during the hunting season, terrestrial influences decidedly preponderated.

She could not help liking smart habits and nice clothes, nor could she refrain from a feeling of triumph when she reflected that her waist with a little squeezing only measured twenty inches round, and that she could tie a tie better than nine hunting men out of ten.

Such facts as these compensated for a good many minor disappointments.

Chief amongst the latter, had been the want of attention hitherto paid to her by Lord Littelbrane.

As a man, she did not care for him one bit, and moreover with that marvellous—

what may fairly be called *husband*—instinct
possessed by the sex, she knew that she
never should.

He exhibited none of those points which
attract a woman.

He was neither handsome, nor good
company, nor miserable, nor mysterious,
nor magnetically sympathetic. He was
just Lord Littelbrane, with fifteen thousand a year, and if he had not been Lord
Littelbrane, everybody would have said
what a dull, stupid, uninteresting little
creature he was, and laughed at him for
giving himself airs.

Although his lordship invariably bowed
to Lady De Fochsey, and sometimes even
went the length of making a remark about
the weather, she was distinctly aware, that
in spite of sundry small overtures on her
side, she had failed to make any impression. Now this knowledge always irritates
a woman, especially if she be young and

pretty, and a flirt. The game may not repay the trouble, but if she can't play it to her mind then she always hankers after it.

This was exactly Lady De Fochsey's case.

Besides, she considered it the "proper thing" to be hand-in-glove with the master, if only because he *was* the master. She could forgive his showing no civility to any other ladies, if he showed it to her. But to be treated exactly the same as the whole tribe of women who hunted with the Morbey Anstead hounds, women who had no pretensions to good looks, who had not an idea of "getting themselves up," who did not wear scarlet jackets and white waistcoats, and whose waists were as flat as pancakes, was exceedingly mortifying. Nay, not only mortifying, but incomprehensible. It went beyond her experience everywhere else. By much flattery and insensibility to downright rudeness, she had contrived to a certain extent to ingratiate herself with the Mutual Adorationites. They all condescended to speak to her, but the desire of her life was to get up a flirtation with Lord Littelbrane, if only for the fun of paying him out for having resisted her charms so long. For that he should have done so was in every way unaccountable. She wanted to see him incorporated among her " tame cats; " then wouldn't she lead him a pretty dance.

CHAPTER XIII.

LOVE BY SELECTION.

WITH the instincts of a thorough coquette Lady De Fochsey slightly slackened her horse's speed, as she overtook Lord Littelbrane. If he wished to join her, he should have the opportunity. Thus thinking, she favoured him to one of her sweetest smiles. It was by no means the first time she had smiled upon him; but she told herself that random smiles were like air-wafted seeds, there was always a chance of their bringing forth fruit.

So she smiled on and on, with all a woman's perseverance, and with all a woman's resolution to turn failure into success. This man's impenetrability had piqued her, otherwise she would never have

troubled her head about him. He was far
too stiff and solemn for her taste. She
liked people who could tell a good story,
who could appreciate one when they heard
it, and who didn't mind calling a spade a
spade. Now, with his lordship it had to
be termed a "trowel," or else an "imple-
ment for digging the earth." She liked fun
and gaiety and amusement, whereas all he
seemed to think about were the "pro-
prieties."

And she was sick to death of them; they
had been dinned into her ears ever since
her girlhood, and Sir Jonathan, in his time,
had frequently waxed eloquent on the
subject.

Lady de Fochsey was a woman to whom
admiration was as the breath of life. But
she possessed a certain amount of worldly
sharpness, and had long since come to the
conclusion that the best way of attracting
men was by amusing them; and if you

amused them, it did not do to be too particular either in your manners or your conversation. She had not a very exalted idea of the male sex, nevertheless she could not do without masculine society, and often weakened her own self-respect in the efforts she made to prove agreeable. She could no more help casting an inviting glance at Lord Littelbrane than she could help being a social butterfly. That glance seemed to say : " Oh ! do come and talk to poor little me. For goodness sake, don't be so stand-off."

Had it not been for his lordship's late feeling of desolation, he might not have construed the look in this manner, but big with his resolution of committing matrimony, he was more amenable to feminine influences. Therefore he responded to Lady De Fochsey's pretty smile, and cantered up to her side. She immediately checked the chestnut's speed.

"Good morning," she exclaimed gaily. "I have not had an opportunity of exchanging a word with you all this long, long time. You seemed determined on ignoring my existence."

He reddened. His conscience pricked him more than was agreeable.

"Now that is positively unkind of you to say such a thing. Of course one can't speak to everybody who comes out hunting, but you," rather clumsily, "you are different."

"Ahem! that's a mercy : it's gratifying to my feelings to find I am not included in the list of people with whom your lordship cannot condescend to hold converse in the hunting field."

The satire was lost upon him ; he only thought her words showed a very proper sense of his position and of the responsibilities entailed by it.

"Oh! Ah! You see there are so many

queer folks come out with these hounds
that one is bound to draw the line somewhere."

"Of course," she answered with fine
irony, "still it is pleasing to find you do
not draw it at me, as I began to suspect.
One has feelings, you know," shooting a
languishing glance at him, "even although
one *is* only a woman."

"I have feelings too," he said solemnly,
looking as grave as an undertaker.

"I'm delighted to hear it, my lord.
Upon my word, there have been times when
I doubted their existence: I should think
they were very uncomfortable ones, judg-
ing from your manner."

"They are rather," he admitted, re-
lapsing into silence. He did not wish to
do anything precipitate, and he thought he
had gone far enough on that tack for the
present. There were just one or two little
points which he wanted to ascertain before

committing himself. Was she a flirt, was
she the least bit " loud," and was that
pretty waist of hers produced by tight-
lacing, or merely the result of natural
slimness? He set his face against women
compressing this particular portion of their
body unduly. It was detrimental to the
future race. When he married, he intended
to marry with one given object in view. On
that point he was quite determined.
Nothing else could have induced him to
sacrifice his bachelor independence. At
forty-six men are apt to regard matrimony
as a dubious pleasure ; they have become
too selfish and too confirmed in their own
habits.

But in spite of her companion's tacitur-
nity, Lady De Fochsey had no intention of
allowing their interview thus soon to come
to an end. So good a chance of inserting
the thin edge of the wedge might not occur
again for a long time. If he would not

talk on one subject she would try another,
a very harmless and innocent one, that
could not possibly frighten him. Perhaps
she had been a little—just a little—too
sarcastic, only she did so long to give him
a good shake, and put some life and
naughtiness into him. He was so frightfully slow and heavy, and yet did not seem
to have the least idea of the fact.

"Dear me!" she exclaimed, reining in
her horse, with a gesture of feminine ex-
haustion. "What a terribly long jog!
How much further is it to the covert?"

She thought it well to ascertain what
time was likely to be accorded her, so as to
make a satisfactory disposition of her
forces.

"Only about a quarter of a mile," he
answered, taking stock of the width of her
chest and the symmetry of her limbs. A
narrow-chested woman would not have met
with his approbation.

" What a comfort! That's the most cheering piece of news I've heard for a long time."

" Are you tired, Lady De Fochsey ? "

" Dreadfully so ; Burnett has been going at such a tremendous pace ; I can't think what has made him in so great a hurry. Poor Little Mayfly," bending forward and patting her horse's neck, " is quite hot."

" And her mistress ? "

" Her mistress is hot too."

" Why don't you walk a little, and take a rest ? " he suggested.

" I can't, I should be left alone, all by myself, miles away from everybody."

" Not if you will let me stay with you."

She turned her blue eyes full upon him. She had never noticed before how weak and watery his colourless ones were, but she softened her voice, and said caressingly :

" *You!* Oh! Lord Littelbrane; you can't be in earnest, surely?"

"Yes," he rejoined, growing bolder. "Why not me as well as another?" and the warm blood rushed up into his faded face, giving it quite an animated expression.

Again she smiled; this time with conscious triumph. Her theory of the seedling had proved correct. A clever woman has only to bide her time, and there are very few men who will escape her. If she has good looks as well, then she can count almost surely on the result.

"You—you are very kind," she said, coyly.

"I think you might trust me a little bit," he said, dropping his voice.

But this was too much for her ladyship's sense of the ridiculous. She laughed out loud.

"I *have* trusted you, Lord Littelbrane, I

have trusted you for the last three years, and hunted regularly with these hounds. Only——" checking herself abruptly.

"Go on," he said impatiently. "Only what?"

"Must I tell you?"

"Yes."

"Then," raising her limpid blue eyes reproachfully to his, "you have never displayed the slightest wish for me to place faith in you until to-day. I have trusted you enormously, but always—from a distance."

He felt flattered. He was not sharp-witted enough to detect the fine sting of irony present in even her prettiest speeches; at all events he chose only to extract the honey.

"Lady De Fochsey," he said, with considerable agitation, "will you promise me something?"

"What is it, my lord? A wise woman

never makes rash promises. She listens first, and promises afterwards."

"Promise that you will trust me from a distance no longer."

She hesitated for a moment—just a pretty little feminine hesitation, calculated to make him more eager. Then, with another swift upward look of the blue eyes, she said demurely:

"It is for you, not me, to decide the distance. You can hardly expect me to make the first advances. Remember, that for these three long years I have always been under the impression you did not like me."

Never had Lady De Fochsey appeared to greater advantage than when she uttered these words.

The air and exercise had brought a rosy flush to her cheeks. Her eyes sparkled with fun, triumph, and excitement, and her neat, upright figure, with its perfectly fitting scarlet coat, swayed voluptuously to and fro, yielding to every movement of her horse. What matter that the captivating golden fringe, which peeped from beneath her hat, was false; or that she was suffering agonies from the pretty little patent leather boot displayed with such extreme liberality? The soul knoweth its own bitterness, and Lord Littelbrane knew nothing of these things. He saw her only as she appeared to the outside world, not as she was and felt to herself.

"Me! Dislike *you !*" he stammered, beginning to wonder at his own indifference. "How could you have entertained so preposterous an idea?"

"I did not know—I—I thought you tried to avoid me."

"Pure imagination, my dear lady. The fact of the matter is, that in my position as master of hounds, it does not do for me to display any active preferences out hunting."

"You have certainly succeeded in concealing them admirably," she interrupted, her love of fun getting the better of her prudence. "No one could possibly have suspected that you entertained any. In fact your avoidance of womankind was almost marked."

"I don't profess to be what is called a lady's man," he said, not without a touch of pride.

"And I am sure that nobody would accuse you of being one," she retorted in her most *agaçante* manner.

"But," he went on, blushing up to the very roots of his hair, "I have always admired you. Always," emphatically. "From the very first."

She burst into a peal of silvery laughter.

"Oh! my lord, you do me too much honour. I am charmed to hear it." And through her vain little frame shot a thrill of triumph.

" 'Pon my soul, it's the truth. You're an awfully nice woman."

" In that case, you must be a very stupid man not to have found it out sooner."

" By Jingo! I believe you are right. You think I have been remiss in my attentions, do you?"

" I did not say so, my lord."

" No, but your words implied it. Come, tell me. Have I not guessed pretty near the mark?" And he sidled up an inch or two nearer to her. It pleased his vanity to think that she had been hankering after him and felt hurt by his non-sociability.

" I will not make any damaging admissions," she responded, " though perhaps," sighing sentimentally, " it may have occurred to me now and again, that you considered women out of place in the hunting field."

"I swear that I never thought any such thing. Why! Lady De Fochsey, I have always looked upon you as one of the chief ornaments of my hunt."

She could not suppress her mirth. It was so irresistibly funny after three whole years to find him wake up all of a sudden, for no apparent rhyme or reason, and begin paying her a series of grave and elaborate compliments. She hardly knew whether he was in earnest or not.

But anyway, she had not the least intention of letting him see how elated she felt. She was far too well versed in the ways of the world to jump down a man's throat who had committed the heinous offence of taking such an unconscionable time in discovering her attractions. True, it was better than not finding them out at all, but he must be made to feel his own stupidity—the pleasures he had missed.

"You will turn my head by so much

adulation," she said demurely. " May I
venture to ask when you first made the
discovery of my being an *ornament* to
your hunt? It must have been extremely
recent."

Her mocking, airy tone disconcerted,
whilst it provoked him. He hated " chaff."
And across his mind dimly crept the idea
that she was " chaffing " *him*.

"I have stated a fact," he said reprov-
ingly, " and you seem to doubt my word.
I don't like sceptical people."

" Quite right," said her ladyship quiz-
zingly. " They are apt to be bores at
times. Nevertheless, I do not think you
need feel surprised at my being a little
slow of belief. It has only just dawned
upon me, that I am an ornament, at all
events in your eyes."

" I suppose you thought me blind,
then? " he said somewhat huffily.

" I am not quite sure. I believe I considered you blind, after the manner of those who won't see. People say that is the worst form of any."

" Well, my eyes are opened at last, at any rate, and I apologise for all my short-comings."

" Don't," she said jestingly. " It would take you such a long time. Besides," shrugging her shoulders with a coquettish gesture, " it really would be too absurd to apologise to me, because it has never entered your head to see anything to admire in me, until to-day."

Her persistent levity had the effect of making him more earnest.

" It by no means follows that a man does not admire a woman because he has not the impudence to tell her so to her face," he said, with some heat.

" Don't you think women very easily forgive that sort of impudence ? " she asked innocently.

" I hardly know."

" Do you suppose *I* would not have forgiven *you*, Lord Littelbrane." And the arrant little flirt looked wickedly round at him with her babyish turquoise eyes.

" Well—perhaps you might," he answered, beginning to feel his head swim, and his heart beat with a strange and unaccustomed sensation.

" Then why didn't you tell me ? "

This was a regular " poser," and he took some time before making any answer. At length he said, with a return to his serious manner :

" I could tell you a good many things if I chose." And he stared straight out over his horse's ears, as if afraid to encounter another glance so full of temptation as the last.

" Do," she said persuasively. " I'm all curiosity."

14*

He looked undecidedly at her for a second, then turned his head away.

"Perhaps I may some day," he responded with growing solemnity, for the immense gravity of the step he had in contemplation weighed upon his spirit like a ton of iron.

If he married, it was from a sense of duty alone, not to gratify his personal inclinations. He was bound to commit matrimony sooner or later, and the lady of his choice was equally bound to be young, healthy and well-bred, in order to bring into the world a desirable number of little Littelbranes. Selection was a thing he had not studied very deeply, but he opined that it should certainly be exercised amongst people in exalted spheres. His own, he considered a very exalted sphere; and therefore the mother of the future heir of Littelbrane Castle was a being not to be chosen from the low standard of human passion, but from the far nobler and loftier one of the influences she was likely to bring to bear upon posterity.

Keeping this laudable object steadily in view, Lord Littelbrane had slowly come to the conclusion that amongst all the ladies of his acquaintance, Lady De Fochsey best fulfilled the necessary conditions.

Eight-and-twenty was an excellent age. Neither too young nor yet too old. The only thing that distressed him, was that she had had no family by her first husband. But then her married life had been short, and Sir Jonathan very ailing and infirm.

Such were his reflections, as, fatigued by the magnitude of the conversational effort already made, he once more relapsed into silence. But he little knew the daring aggressive nature of the woman with whom he had to deal. Lady De Fochsey had long since recognized him as one of those men who must be " talked to." She found it up-hill work, but much practice had rendered her equal to the occasion.

"A penny for your thoughts!" she exclaimed, after a prolonged pause, during which she had been stealthily studying her companion's face, and thinking how terribly vapid and dull its owner was. He started and turned red at being thus attacked.

"At that particular moment I was wondering whether you ever felt lonely," he said simply.

She forgave him his stupidity, since she had been occupying his brain.

"Sometimes," she said, putting on a pensive air. "But why do you ask. Do you?"

"Frightfully, since poor dear Harry died. I don't know that I can go on living by myself much longer. I begin to want a companion very badly indeed."

Lady De Fochsey was an audacious little person, and had the gift of saying the boldest things in the most innocent and artless of manners.

" If that is so, Lord Littelbrane, why on earth do you not get married ? Everybody says that you ought to."

" Do they ? " he inquired, flushing crimson.

" Yes, everybody. Is there no one you like well enough to make your wife ? "

" Yes," he said slowly. " I—I—think— there—is."

" Ah ! I thought so. And pray, who may the lucky lady be ? "

Something in the expression of his coun-tenance made her heart palpitate. A strange thought flashed through her mind. A thought full of gratified vanity, but without one particle of sentiment in its composition.

IIe turned quite pale, opened his lips as if to say something, when alas ! alas ! a loud tally-ho came ringing through the air.

In another moment they were engulfed by a galloping crowd, and borne far apart.

"Was there ever anything so provoking?" said Lady De Fochsey to herself. "I do believe he meant to propose. And oh, what fun it would have been, and what a feather in my cap!"

As for Lord Littelbrane, the perspiration had gathered in great beads upon his noble brow. He wiped it hastily away, and uttered a sigh which seemed torn from the very depths of his being.

"By Jove!" he muttered, "making love is awful work, worse even than I thought. It would have been all over with me in another minute. I was going ahead so deuced fast." Then he shook his head, and murmured disapprovingly: "Too fast —too fast by a great deal. It's just as well that fox went away when he did.

Now I can take another week or two to make up my mind, and think the matter over."

He had no doubts about Lady De Fochsey. It never occurred to him to imagine that if he condescended to ask, she was not prepared to accept with pleasure.

CHAPTER XIV.

ALTHOUGH it was now nearly three o'clock, and sportsmen had already indulged in one good gallop, it had by no means abated their keenness. After the long summer's inactivity, they were full of ardour, which even the blindness of the country could not keep in check.

They were just as eager to pursue this second fox as they had been to follow the first, and he took them along at a very fair pace; though after the first ten minutes were over he showed himself in his true colours, and turned out a faint-hearted, twisty brute. This fact, however, did not in the least detract from Bob's pleasure.

He was far too much of a novice at the
game to care whether hounds ran straight,
or round and round in a ring. It was all
the same to him, as long as they kept
moving on, and he could get plenty of
jumping. The jumping, indeed, constituted
his chief delight. He thought far more of
it than of fox and hounds. They were
quite subordinate considerations, as com-
pared with the glorious and intoxicating
sensation of feeling yourself up in the air
and never knowing in exactly what fashion
you would descend to the earth. There
was an element of danger in the whole
business which gave it a special charm.
One moment your heart was in your
mouth; the next, words failed to express
the sudden elation which took possession
of every faculty, and made the pulses thrill
with ecstasy. But The Swell and his rider
were no longer so exactly of the same
mind as they had been earlier in the day.

That fastidious animal began to consider that his powers had been quite sufficiently exerted. He was too wise and old a hunter to love jumping for jumping's sake. He looked upon every unnecessary leap as an indignity to his understanding, and grew more and more sulky in consequence.

His late master had almost invariably ridden him first horse, and sent him home early. The cunning creature could not see the fun of being kept out so long, and hankered after his comforting warm mash and good old oats. His buoyancy and spirits departed. It was almost with a feeling of resentment that he turned his head away from home, and for the second time joined in the chase. His ill-humour soon became evident. He no longer fenced as faultlessly as in the morning. One or two places he nogotiated quite slovenly, crashing right in amongst the thorns and binders with his hind-legs.

So badly indeed did he behave, that Bob, as he sailed down at a big hedge, newly plashed, with a very blind ditch on the near side, into which all the lopped-off twigs had been cast, deemed it advisable to rouse him up a little bit. The Swell resented the process and the manner in which it was done. He missed those subtle touches of hand and heel to which he was accustomed. His mouth was fine and very sensitive.

Bob gave it a job, and the horse immediately tossed up his head, with the result that he almost put both fore-feet into the ditch, and only succeeded in getting over with a desperate flounder, which landed him on his knees.

Crack, crack, rang an awful report in Bob's ears as he was jerked violently forwards, and then nearly as violently back, whilst The Swell righted himself, grunting with terror and indignation. His unhappy rider knew what had happened.

He needed not to be told. The disaster which he feared, with almost morbid fear, had taken place at last. He glanced hurriedly at his nether limbs.

Yes, there they were! Those two abominable elastic straps, dangling down about a quarter of a yard in length, from the hem of his trousers. One of them had even a little square bit of cloth still sticking to it, which proved that the wrench must have been considerable. An unutterable horror seized him. A kind of sinking shame. And yet he did not realize the full extent of his misfortunes until he had galloped half-way across a fifty-acre field.

Then he began to feel odious and horrible sensations of discomfort. They seemed to come creeping slowly, slowly upward and to run all along his spine. Warm as he was, a shudder passed through his frame. He tried not to look downwards, but a species of fascination forced him to do so.

Unhappy young man! The man who had fancied himself superior to clothes, and who affected to despise boots and breeches. What did he see, you ask?

He saw two inches of white leg—disgustingly white, that made the matter so much worse — fully exposed to public vision; whilst his stockings had wriggled themselves into the heels of his boots, and his trousers were up to his knees. Pitiable spectacle! With the agony of desperation, he tried to pull the one up and the other down. It afforded only temporary relief. The wretched things would not stop in their place. And all this time hounds were running well, even if not at a furious pace. Had there been a gate close by he would have hailed it with joy, and hidden his diminished head amongst the roadsters. But there was none. For once Stiffshire failed to supply the desired commodity. He *must* go on riding, and he *must* go on jumping, whether he liked it or not.

Overwhelmed with confusion, all of a sudden he heard a loud guffaw. Turning sharply round in the saddle, he perceived, carefully crawling through a handy gap, no less a person than his old antagonist, General Prosieboy. That man seemed to have a knack of turning up on every occasion, just when he was least wanted. At the present moment he was evidently gloating over Bob's discomfiture. His fat old sides literally shook with laughter, whilst his face assumed a deeper and more purple hue than its wont. Perhaps Bob was unreasonable ; but the sight of the old gentleman simply maddened him. It seemed to set every nerve quivering and throbbing, and added a thousand times to his distress. He would have given a hundred pounds at that moment to have been able to punch General Prosieboy's head. There was a murderous instinct within him, which, if not quelled, might lead to terrible results.

Clapping spurs into The Swell he fled precipitately, as the only way of escaping from his tormentor.

But whither?

He did not think—he did not care, so long as he was somewhere near the hounds, and away from the rest of the field.

For five whole minutes he rode like a madman; cramming his horse at all sorts of break-neck places, now crashing into a bull-finch, anon scrambling over fences, again smashing recklessly through timber. The Swell had never been so utterly amazed and disgusted in the whole course of his career. His legs were a pincushion. They were stuck full of thorns, his sides were dark with crimson gore, and a long red scratch disfigured the stifle of his near hind leg. To look at him, he might have been

a miserable hireling, whose rider was bent
on having his two guineas' worth to the
very last farthing.

Presently Bob grew calmer. For a
hasty backward glance had shown him
that not a soul was following in his footsteps. All he wanted was to get away
from the crowd, and to escape their gibes
and jeers.

But before long, his thoughts took a
different turn. He began to imagine that
he was entirely alone with hounds. It
never struck him to look to the right or to
the left. His eyes were fixed on the light
vanishing sterns ahead. Even the recollec-
tion of those two white legs faded from his
mind, erased by the imaginary glories of his
position. Neither was excitement wanting.
For none can be greater than that of riding
a well-nigh beaten horse at a succession of
big fences, and counting surely on a fall at
each one. A man's courage is severely

tested then—more perhaps than at any other time.

With all his good qualities, The Swell was not a *bonâ fide* stayer.

He could live through a really fast run, first thing in the morning when he came out fresh and well, but although it might take some time to discover the fact, he was a cur at heart. For if he once got ever so little pumped, he never came again that day.

The morning gallop had stretched his girths quite as much as he deemed fit. After five and thirty to forty minutes, a twenty-pound screw would have carried a man almost as well to hounds for the remainder of the afternoon.

Besides which natural idiosyncrasies, he had not been out hunting this season and was a little short of condition, like most gentlemen's horses early in November. Bob, however, was not sufficiently ex-

15*

perienced to take these things into consideration. He had a good deal to learn yet,
before becoming a finished cross-country
performer. The number of jumps you have
jumped, does not constitute the sole glory
of fox-hunting, as before long he was
destined to discover. Wise is he, who,
nursing his horse, looks upon leaping
simply as a means to an end.

All of a sudden, straight in front of him,
Bob saw the gleam of water peeping coldly
out from amongst a fringe of low, stunted
willows. As he did so, Matthews' words
recurred to him: " He has but one fault,
sir. He won't face water."

But he—Bob—was in that state of sur-
excitation, when he flattered himself that a
really resolute person on The Swell's back was
bound to make all the difference. Because
a horse refused to look at a brook with one
man, he might be persuaded or forced to
have it with another. Anyhow, he would

not show the white feather, even although he believed there was no one to see what he was about. But his own self-respect shrank from the idea of " funking." Physical cowardice inspired him with a supreme contempt. As for the hounds— well, he forgot to notice whether they had actually crossed the brook or not. He *thought* they were going to, and that was enough. He never observed how old True-tongue paused on the very brink, and then feathered along the side. Instead of closely watching her movements, he caught his horse by the head, and drove him at the water, just as hard as ever he could.

To his surprise, he found on approaching the brook, that it was bigger than he suspected. Should that alter his determination ? Certainly not.

He raised his whip hand. The Swell swerved away from it; and then—oh, horror ! he felt him begin to collapse under him. He dug the spurs into the poor beast's sides and kept him as straight as he could. He held him in such an iron grasp that he thought the horse was bound to make a bid for it. Not he !

In the very last stride, The Swell stopped dead short, stretched out his neck, lowered his head and gazed in mute obstinacy at the dark depths beneath him. He knew what they felt like. He had tried them once, long ago in his early youth, and had made a mental resolve never, by any chance, to renew their acquaintance. Some might like cold water. *He* did not approve of it. The dry system appeared to him to possess insuperable advantages. And Bob? the rash youth who thought his will was stronger than that of the animal he bestrode, and who did not know that a horse, when he is in earnest, can defy any man ever born ! Well, Bob simply flew over his head, like an arrow shot from a bow, and descended plump into the midst of the stream. It was awfully deep ! He went right down to the bottom, rolled about in the soft mud, and imbibed more water than he had ever done before or hoped to do again. Gasping and spluttering, he rose to the surface, making frantic endeavours to regain his footing. Roars of laughter greeted his reappearance—real, unfeigned, hearty laughter.

It seemed to him, in that never-to-be-forgotten moment, which crowned all his previous mishaps, as if the whole of the Morbey Anstead Field were congregated on the banks of this fatal brook, and were unanimous in regarding his involuntary immersion as a most excellent joke. If he could have felt any sensations of heat, he would have grown hot with indignation. Even The Swell turned his full blue eye upon him with an air of amiable triumph, which seemed to say : " Ah ! you would have done much better to have taken my advice."

It was a terrible thing, having to scramble out on to *terra firma* before all those laughing faces. Nobody appeared to possess the least instinct of pity. Even Lady De Fochsey, his quondam ally, was smiling broadly and was evidently greatly amused.

Poor Bob stood and shook himself like a Newfoundland dog. The water poured from his ears and saturated clothes. The glory of the day had departed. The sky had clouded over, a cold wind arose which whistled across the uplands. He felt chilled to the bone. And then, all at once, a gruff voice from amongst the crowd said :

"I say, young fellow, how are the legs ? They look whiter than ever after getting such a real good washing. It will save your soap, anyway."

This sally was received with much tittering and applause.

Bob could have sworn the voice belonged to General Prosieboy, but he failed to perceive that gentleman's whereabouts. Perhaps it was lucky for his grey hairs. It is the last straw which breaks the camel's back.

Bob had endured a good deal, on this memorable day, from the hands of the Mutual Adorationites! He now felt as if he could endure no more. His wet clothes clung heavily about him and weighed like a ton. Without saying a word he clambered laboriously up into the saddle, and rode straight off in the direction of home. Any temporary feeling of elation had been destroyed by his cold bath. A more crestfallen, dejected and miserable young man, it would have been impossible to find in all Her Majesty's possessions. Just when he was particularly anxious to make a favourable *début* in the hunting field, he had contrived to tumble off and provide amusement for every one present. The tears almost started to his eyes. He felt so bitterly humiliated. Swearing was not a habit he greatly approved of, but oh! how he swore at those "confounded" straps, which, rightly or wrongly, he looked upon as the chief cause of his disasters.

CHAPTER XV.

As soon as he succeeded in reaching the first road, Bob set off at a swinging trot. His teeth were chattering, and his limbs frozen. To make matters worse the wind increased, till it seemed to blow through his clothes as if they were paper, and chilled the very marrow in his bones. Under these circumstances, it was perhaps excusable that he displayed but little regard for The Swell's fore-legs, and went pounding along at a tremendous pace. After he had gone about a couple of miles, he saw a poor old labourer engaged in the tedious task of breaking stones by the road-side.

Then for the first time it occurred to him, that for aught he knew, he might be going wrong, since he was by no means sure of the way. Therefore, checking his tired horse, he asked: "Is this right for Straightem Court, my man?"

"Yes, sir, quite right, sir," came the reply. "Keep straight on till you pass Killerton village, then turn sharp to the right, through a bridle-gate, that takes you across the fields almost into Straightem. It'ull save you a couple of miles if not more."

"But how am I to find the bridle-gate?" inquired Bob, intent on making sure of his directions.

"You can't possibly mistake it, sir, because there's a sign-post within five yards."

Moved to compassion by the feeble old man's shrunken frame, hollow cheeks and half-starved appearance, Bob fumbled in his waistcoat pocket until he found a shilling.

" Thank you," he said kindly. " There
—take this. I have no doubt that it will
do you a great deal more good than it will
me."

The recipient's blessings followed him as
he rode away, and for a few minutes he
reflected gravely on the miserable condition
of an honest man like the one he had just
left, when age and infirmity combined to
render the struggle against poverty more
and more difficult. What could life mean
to him? Only a weary, weary warring
against cold and wind and rain; against
hunger and fatigue; without amusement,
without pleasure; without comfort of any
sort. A dreary existence at best, but
rendered a thousand times more so by
failing health, and the pains of a poor,
worn-out old body. The body! Ah!
what a drag and torment it was to human
beings! If only they could rise above it!
And yet even a simple toothache could

dethrone the greatest genius from its seat.
Brain, psychic force : of what did they
avail, when Pain could lay them in the
dust so easily and ride triumphant over
them ? Their very defeat only served to
prove the weakness and mortality of man.

But Bob's meditations were cut short by
a fresh calamity. The road had been
newly mended and was covered with
stones. The Swell toed them with the
carelessness of a weary animal. Suddenly
he trod on a loose flint, and immediately
afterwards went dead lame. So lame
indeed that trotting was out of the
question. It was as much as he could do
to walk.

Bob's star was clearly not in the
ascendant to-day. He thought that he
had already reached the limits of his ill-
luck. He found there was still a margin
which had not entered into his calculations.
The Swell's small ears now bobbed up and

down with torturing irregularity. They made him feel like a monster of cruelty.

Dismounting, he proceeded to examine the poor beast's foot, but could perceive nothing to account for his sudden lameness. In truth, it would have taken a pretty powerful magnifying glass to have detected that small, sharp piece of granite, which having penetrated the frog, was causing such exquisite agony.

Being now forced to travel at a foot's pace, Bob considered it was warmer walking than riding, besides he could not help being sorry for the unhappy animal, whose appearance had undergone such a total transformation since he sallied forth in the morning, champing at his bit, arching his glossy neck and playfully whisking his tail. There was not a symptom of light-heartedness left now.

The unfortunate Swell no longer merited he name. Anything less like an equine

dandy could not have been imagined.   His
sleek bay coat was hard and white with
dry perspiration, his sides were disfigured
by spur marks, his legs incrusted with mud ;
whilst his eye wore a dull, glazy look,
which told of physical discomfort.   If to
him had been given the gift of speech, he
would probably have said : " My master
may be ' plucky,' but never let me see him
again—never let me have anything more to
do with him.   He has ridden my tail off."

Bob trudged sturdily on, till at length
he reached Killerton village, and the bridle-
gate beyond.   Then, when once more a
vista of green fields refreshed his eyes, he
remounted, thinking that the probabilities
were The Swell would go less tender on the
soft, springy grass.

In this supposition he was correct, nevertheless it was a weary ride home, cold and
slow and miserable.   The sort of ride which
effectually obliterates any pleasant impres-

sions left by the day's sport, and which makes a man begin to ask himself whether fox-hunting repays the many disappointments and discomforts that must necessarily come in its train.

It was a bad thing for Bob, on his very first acquaintance with the noble pastime, to have arrived at such a stage, but, as before stated, physical misery soon makes a different creature of man, and quickly subdues him.

Our hero followed the track as well as he could, and his spirits slightly revived. But after a time, the path disappeared, swallowed up in a sea of grass, and then he had to trust entirely to his bump of locality —a bump which he did not possess in as large a degree as might have been expected.

Besides, it is by no means an easy thing to thread one's way through a series of narrow gates, in an entirely new country.

These huge uninhabited pastures, for which Stiffshire is celebrated all over the hunting world, and which constitute its glory and its renown, are desolate in the extreme. You may go for miles and miles without meeting anything but herds of grazing cattle, woolly sheep, and an occasional rough young colt. The cloud-shadows race across these vast stretches of undulating verdure, and the wind sweeps over them at its icy will. There are scarcely any trees to break its fury. Only a few isolated specimens in the hedgerows, which rear their gaunt, stunted arms to the dull sky, as if imploring that their lives may be granted them. Here and there a great black bullfinch, situated on the summit of some rising hill, lies like a long dark wall against the grey horizon. A magpie flits across the path. Intersected lines of fences break up the green, rendering it yet more vivid—and this is Stiffshire. Lonely, silent, sullen, undecked by the beauties of Nature, yet withal not destitute of a certain grandeur, born of her vastness and her desolation. A solitary country, that after a time possesses a kind of weird charm for the solitary soul that walks the earth alone. Bob looked about him. Far as eye could reach, not a human habitation was within vision. He began to experience fresh misgivings as to the route. Sometimes the fields were so large that they had two or three gates, and then he was just obliged to guess at the most likely one. But he might have gone wrong a dozen times over, and as the afternoon advanced, would have been many degrees easier in his mind, could he but have reached a road. Many and many a time did he regret having left one. He would not have grudged the greater ᐧ distance, for the sense of extra security conferred. Already it seemed to him as if he had been hours on his way.

All of a sudden, just when he was set-
tling down into a state of melancholy resig-
nation, he perceived a brand new gate,
painted white, about fifty yards ahead.
And through the bars of this gate, he saw
the moist road glimmering, as the young
crescent moon, high up aloft, reflected her
pallid face in a little pool of water. Joy-
fully he hastened his steps, whilst even The
Swell pricked his ears, and seemed to know
he was nearing home.

Bob stretched out his arm, and tried to
lift up the latch with the crook of his
hunting crop. It was secured by some
new-fangled process which he did not
understand, and yielded not an inch. He
made another essay with the same result,
another and yet another. Then The Swell
grew impatient, and pushed heavily against
the barrier with his strong chest. Finding
it still closed, he lurched away from it in
disgust, as much as to say, " It is for you

to open this, not me. I've done my best,
now you do yours."

Bob did all he could to coax him up to
the gate again. He tried patting, he tried
speaking, he tried spurring. But the horse
refused with all the obstinacy of which
brute nature is capable. In little, as in
big things, The Swell would try once, but
never more often. He was like some men
and many women—easily disheartened by
failure, and let failure conquer *him*, instead
of *he* conquering failure.

This delay proved most vexatious. For
when you have been immersed in a brook,
on a cold November afternoon, every
minute appears of consequence. Your
whole soul hankers after warmth, and a
dry change of clothes. There was nothing
for it, however, but to get off. Bob
did so, and throwing the reins over his
bridle arm, proceeded to ascertain why
this particular gate was unlike all other

gates, and refused to allow itself to be opened.

But heaving, pushing, lifting—all proved useless. At the end of five minutes he was in despair. Finally he put his shoulder to the refractory bars, and tried to break them down by main force. He was a strong, athletic young fellow, six feet in height, and broad of chest, with muscles developed by the healthy open-air life he had led. But he was just as powerless against those strong white timbers as a child of six. He could not even bend them, although he put forth all his strength, and his face turned scarlet with exertion.

A heavy sigh escaped from him. It acknowledged his defeat. Totally disconcerted, he told himself that he must retrace his footsteps and seek some fresh means of entering the road. He glanced at the fence which ran on either side of the gate.

But it was perfectly unjumpable, and even had it been otherwise, he doubted very much whether The Swell, in his present state, could have made an effort. He was at his wit's end. And then, all at once hope surged up into his heart.

He heard a noise, the clatter of hoofs approaching on the hard macadam. Thank goodness! help was at hand. The people of the country would surely understand how these mysterious gates opened. And even if the worst came to the worst, with the aid of another good, strong man, he felt confident that he could break the wretched thing down. It would be easy to pay for the damages afterwards, but home, sweet home, was the chief consideration just at present.

Bob's disappointment was therefore extreme, when a sharp turn in the road revealed a young lady, riding a smart dun cob, about fourteen hands high.

Their eyes met, and she seemed immediately to guess the cause of his distress. She blushed a little, hesitated for a moment, and then pulled the dun up to a stand.

"I see you are in difficulties," she said, in a voice whose frank, straightforward tones impressed him favourably. "Will you allow me to help you?"

In his amazement at this slim, slip of a girl imagining that she could open a gate which had defied all his own energies, Bob did a very rude thing.

He made no answer, but simply stood still, and stared at the fair Samaritan who thus kindly volunteered to assist him.

END OF VOL. I.